Ross stood against the door, watching her

He was thinner, and there were lines deeply etched from cheek to jaw, giving him a bitter, almost cynical appearance. His mouth, too, had a grim twist to it, and the gray eyes were hard and unyielding. He was the same, yet so very, very different.

"Ross," she breathed, and in a second she was across the room, sliding her arms around his waist, pressing herself against him with all the pent-up longing of the past eighteen months.

"Oh, Ross—" she choked. "I thought you were dead!" And as the tears welled and overflowed, she pressed her face into his neck. It was ecstasy to hold him like this, sheer joy just to be with him again.

"No doubt you would have preferred it if I were," he said.

PAMELA HATTON says her own life has been pretty romantic so far. She met her husband when she was fifteen, and he proposed six weeks later, convinced that they would marry. They now have two sons, who are as persistent as their father. When Pamela left full-time teaching to bring up her sons, her husband persuaded her to send off her first literary effort. When her second attempt was accepted, he bought her a word processor and told her to get on with it—though he hadn't read any of her stories. Swimming, landscape planning and gardening, and renovating their country home in England are included in their hobbies.

PAMELA HATTON

remember tomorrow

Harlequin Books

TORONTO • NEW YORK • LONDON
AMSTERDAM • PARIS • SYDNEY • HAMBURG
STOCKHOLM • ATHENS • TOKYO • MILAN

Harlequin Presents first edition December 1989
ISBN 0-373-11226-2

Original hardcover edition published in 1989
by Mills & Boon Limited

CHAPTER ONE

CASSIE heard the phone ringing as she put her key in the lock and gave a groan of irritation. The flight from Paris had been delayed by fog, and, after oversleeping and then rushing her breakfast with Mandy and David, she had raced to the airport, only to spend hours kicking her heels in a freezing airport lounge. The drive into London through the Saturday evening traffic hadn't improved matters, and what she wanted now above anything else was to relax in a hot bath before crawling into bed for an early night. As she fumbled with her key she hoped fervently that the call was for Natalie, who she knew would still be at the boutique, or, better still, a wrong number, but as she hurried down the hall and snatched the receiver from its cradle she was doomed to disappointment. The voice at the other end was all too familiar.

'Cassie! Where on earth have you been? I've been trying to get in touch with you for days!'

'Hello, Mummy.' She should have guessed, she thought. She was only surprised her mother hadn't sent out a search party before now. She wedged the receiver between her shoulder and chin as she peeled off her gloves. 'I've been away for a few days. I've only just this minute got back——'

'You've been away? Without telling us?'

'Natalie knew where I was——'

'You mean you told those friends of yours what you were doing and never thought to mention it to your family?' Elaine Brett's voice was brittle with accusation.

'All you had to do was phone the boutique,' Cassie pointed out, but her words were drowned by her mother's furious outburst.

'I couldn't get through to the boutique! And when I did all they'd tell me was that you weren't in and Natalie Peers was *unavailable*!'

'Mummy——'

'And not only that, Neil has been out of his mind!'

Cassie stiffened. 'Neil?'

'Yes, *Neil*. I would have thought if you'd told anyone you were going away you would have told Neil!'

Neil was the reason she'd gone away in the first place, Cassie thought acidly; Neil McAllister and his pompous attitude. That last evening had been the final straw. She could see his face now: his outraged features, his determination to make her see *his* point of view—and all because she'd told him about Natalie's offer of a partnership. He had informed her—in no uncertain terms—that he had another kind of partnership in mind, and while he had no objections to Cassie's, as he put it, 'playing at business' before their marriage, there would be no question of her working afterwards. And anyway, he had added matter-of-factly, she would be far too busy helping him with his entertaining, and later, bringing up his babies! She had sat through it all in thunderous silence. The possibility of marriage with Neil was something she had only briefly considered, and his calm assumption that her marriage to him was a certainty, and that that certainty gave him the right to organise her life for her now had precipitated a furious row, which in turn had precipitated her packing her bags and leaving for Paris, taking up Natalie's offer of a holiday while she made up her mind about the partnership. She'd needed a breathing space, she realised now. Time to herself to think things through, to think her future through—but now it seemed she'd walked right back to where she'd started from.

'And why would I tell Neil what my plans were?' she asked now, and she heard her mother's hiss of frustration at the other end.

'Because—well, because—oh, Cassie! You know what I mean...' Her mother sounded almost petulant now.

'No, I don't know what you mean,' Cassie retorted crisply. 'Perhaps you'd care to explain it to me some time?'

'Oh, Cassie! Just because you had a silly row with him——'

'A silly row?' Cassie was finding it difficult to control her own temper now. 'Is that what he told you it was? A silly row?'

'Neil only wants what's best for you, darling, as do we all...'

Cassie collapsed into the chair behind her with a muffled exclamation. That was the whole point—what *was* best for her? Marriage to Neil? Just because he was her stepfather's right-hand man in the firm, because he was expected to inherit Brett's Engineering—was that how her mother's mind was working? Didn't she know it was still too soon, too soon after Ross?

She stared bleakly up at the ceiling. She'd had a nightmare again last night—that was why she'd overslept this morning. She been awake half the night, terrified to go back to sleep, terrified of being alone, and

Mandy had sat with her. It was psychological, Mandy had said, because she was under pressure. Pressure from Neil, pressure from her mother and stepfather...but that didn't make the pain inside her any easier to bear. She could still recall the vivid details. She'd been with Ross in the car, feeling him warm and solid beside her, and then slowly had come that feeling of speed, the screeching tyres, the vicious bends, the horror of those oncoming lights—would it haunt her for ever? Would *Ross* haunt her for ever?

She closed her eyes for a moment. Her head was beginning to ache and she wished her mother would get to the point. 'What did you want to tell me, Mummy?' she sighed resignedly.

'Cassandra, there's no need to take that tone of voice with me,' Elaine sniffed. 'However, you're right, we'll save this particular discussion for another day; my head's beginning to ache——'

'*Your* head's aching?'

'Cassie, you've no idea what it's been like these last few days!'

'What's wrong? Has Roddy gone off on one of his binges again?' Cassie murmured coolly as she began to undo the buttons on her coat.

'*Cassandra!*' To Cassie's surprise she heard her mother's voice break on what sounded suspiciously like a sob. 'That's no way to talk about your brother-in-law, and no, he isn't on one of his binges! In fact, Roddy and Julia are staying here, with James and I, and I think it would be best if you came to stay too, just in case...'

'Just in case—what?' Cassie sat up, feeling the hairs on the back of her neck beginning to prickle uneasily. 'What's wrong, Mummy? What's happened?'

'It's your grandfather...'

Now she knew her mother was finding it difficult to control her voice, and a flicker of alarm made her fingers tighten on the receiver. 'Grandfather Brett? He's not ill?'

'He's in hospital—undergoing surgery—I'm phoning from the hospital now——'

'Oh, God!' Cassie collapsed back against the chair, her mind suddenly blank with shock.

'It's his heart...' Her mother's voice was muffled. 'He collapsed at the dinner-table...'

'Which hospital is he in?' Cassie demanded, jumping to her feet again. Her car keys were still lying next to the telephone where she'd thrown them and now she reached for them automatically as she made a mental note of her mother's directions. Her gloves were forgotten as she raced out to the car again, her mind fully occupied now with the need to get to the hospital and see for herself just what sort of a state Grandfather Brett was in.

Her mind was full of pictures, pictures of Alexander Brett as she had seen him only a few weeks ago, looking as he had always looked: tall, broad, strong, the blue eyes still sparkling under the heavy brows despite his sixty-nine years. As a child those eyes had terrified the life out of her. He had seemed like a great mountain of a man, and that first impression had remained with her through the years. He was indestructible; it seemed absurd that he should be ill, weak, possibly dying.

The wintry afternoon was darkening into evening and Cassie switched the windscreen wipers on as the first drops of rain splattered against the windscreen. By the time she'd parked the car the rain was falling heavily and, unwilling to waste time searching for her umbrella in the boot, she pulled her collar up and made a dash for it, pausing for a moment in the busy, brightly lit hospital foyer to catch her breath and get her bearings.

She knew her mother and James were in a waiting area on the second floor, and as the lift was already in use she made determinedly for the stairs, running quickly up one, then two flights. She emerged into a dimly lit corridor and hesitated, glancing uncertainly from right to left. The corridor was blank, with a row of anonymous doors, but there was a well-lit area at one end and the figure of a nurse just disappearing round the corner. Unaware that she was almost running, Cassie hurried after the blue-clad figure.

She round the corner only to give a cry of startled surprise as she collided painfully with a wheelchair. She was knocked off balance, sent sprawling across the lap of its occupant, but before she could gather her scattered wits long fingers had gripped her upper arms and she was propelled upwards and backwards, almost thrust away again, so that she staggered back against the wall.

She only just managed to save herself from sliding ignominiously to the floor, but then the pain of her bruised shins—everything—was forgotten as she stared at the man in the wheelchair, and her body went rigid with shock. She felt the blood drain from her face as eyes as cold and grey as the winter sky raked her from head to foot; and then, before she could move or speak, he was gone, swallowed up by the lift, and she stared at the blank face of the lift doors as though she had seen a ghost.

With an effort she pulled herself together and straightened away from the wall. Her limbs were trembling with reaction now, but she turned and began to run back the way she had come, down the corridor to the stairs, stumbling in her haste and grasping the handrail to stop herself careering headlong down the steep stairwell. She raced out into the foyer again, oblivious of staring, startled faces, and made for the entrance, emerging into the rain again just in time to hear the slam of car doors as a car began to pull away from the kerb. She threw herself after it, banging on the window as though demented, but the man in the back seemed to look right through her, the grey eyes as icy as the rain which was plastering her hair to her head and running in rivulets down her neck. Her lips formed his name, but the car pulled away into the traffic, and she was left standing in the gutter, watching its red rear lights disappearing into the darkness.

She felt a touch on her arm and turned, as if in a dream, to find one of the hospital porters at her side.

'Are you all right, miss?'

She stared at him, her green eyes huge in her white face. 'It was Ross,' she said, in a clear high voice. And before he could make a move to catch her she had fallen at his feet in a dead faint.

She regained consciousness in a cubicle in the Outpatients department. She was confused, disorientated, and it only seemed to add to the nightmarish quality of it all; and then her mother was there, demanding to know what had happened, and James, taking control in his usual bluff fashion, ordering a taxi and insisting she be taken home and put straight to bed.

'It's the shock,' she heard him say, and she put her hands over her wet face in silent agony.

Yes, she thought hollowly, that's what it must be. The shock.

She was made to stay in bed all Sunday morning, alone with her thoughts, curiously isolated from the rest of the household. Only Elaine came in to see her, remarking cryptically that she looked better and demanding to be told what had happened.

'I fainted,' Cassie supplied simply, but her mother's stare was almost unnervingly intent.

'You've never fainted in your life!'

'I'd been travelling all day. It was probably the shock, as James said.' Cassie met her mother's look head-on, but that unflickering stare was too much for her and she looked away again.

'Mmm . . . perhaps you're right,' Elaine murmured thoughtfully, still watching her. She seemed about to add something else, but she obviously changed her mind, for she stood up instead and moved to the door. 'Well, take it easy today, darling. Remember, dinner is at six-thirty as usual.' And she went out.

Dinner at six-thirty as usual, Cassie echoed silently, and slid back against the pillows. It seemed strange somehow to be back in James's house. When she had woken up this morning, back in her old bedroom, it had seemed as though the last two years had never happened, as though they had been wiped away by some quirk of time and she was young again, untried, looking forward to simple things like holidays and Christmas. It was just after Christmas when she had first met Ross, at one of Julia's parties, affairs which she had always found so stifling. But then, she and Julia had never really had the same friends.

She'd seen Ross almost as soon as she walked through the door. There had been something about his tall, lean-hipped frame with that topping of dark, curling hair—a certain masculinity, a male charisma, that had immediately drawn her eyes, and, almost as though he could feel her eyes on his back, he had turned and smiled at her.

As the evening progressed she had begun to fear that a smile was all she was going to get from this disturbing stranger, but then he had been there, blocking her path, and even now she could feel that sudden breathlessness as she had looked up into those devastating grey eyes, and the sheer thrill of his long fingers against her skin as they began to dance.

He had suggested they leave, take a drive, and she had willingly agreed, no thought of refusal in her head. She hadn't even known his name at that point.

Of course, she'd been out with boys before, but nothing like this—and Ross was certainly no boy. He was older than her by nearly ten years, she had guessed that first evening, although he wasn't as old as Neil. She'd been out with Neil, too, a few times by then, for dinner or to an occasional show, but with Ross, right from the beginning, it was something completely different.

Love at first sight, she realised later. In the magical weeks and months that followed she had been eager to discover everything about him, surprised to learn just how much they had in common. They listened to the same kind of music, read the same kind of books, both liked swimming and tennis, and she gradually began to realise that she had found in Ross everything she had ever wanted in a man. Incredibly, too, it seemed he had found in her everything he wanted in a woman...

With sudden determination Cassie threw back the covers and climbed out of bed. If she sat still any longer she'd go mad, she thought in desperation. It was too soon to get dressed for dinner, but she could at least have a bath and wash her hair. She went through to the adjoining bathroom and turned the taps fully on, adding bath oil and watching as it foamed and diluted, filling the bathroom with its fragrance.

As she straightened from the side of the bath she caught her full-length reflection in the mirrored tiles on the opposite wall. Tall and slim, she had never developed the more voluptuous curves of her mother and Julia, and, unlike Julia too, she had the fair hair of her father, with just a hint of auburn in its depths. She slipped the straps of her nightdress off her shoulders and let it fall in a silent heap at her feet, surveying her naked reflection with impassive eyes. Long legs topped by a narrow waist, then gently swelling again to accommodate firm, round breasts. She put her hands up and covered her nipples, then slid them slowly down over the smooth skin of her stomach. How many times had Ross's hands followed that same sensuous path?

She closed her eyes on a sudden surge of painful longing. Oh, God, *oh, God*!

She had thought all these sensations—all this frustrated yearning—had been buried long ago, but last night seemed to have brought it all surging back. But Ross was dead—*dead*!

She opened her eyes again and reached for the bathrobe on the back of the door, pulling it around her with trembling fingers and bending to the taps again, struggling to concentrate on the rising water.

Something inside her had shrunk from telling anyone about last night. After all, her family—especially Elaine—had never really approved of Ross. And besides, what could she say? That she thought she'd seen a ghost? Her mouth twisted as she turned the taps off. They'd say she was demented—or worse. They'd say she was mistaken, except that she knew she wasn't. This had been no quick glance at a passing stranger; she had touched him, seen his face, and she knew Ross's features as well as she knew her own. How could she forget those eyes, those hands . . . ? She shook her head, trying to rid herself of those remembered longings, and then abruptly she stepped out of the robe and into the bath, submerging herself completely in the warm, fragrant water.

Later, bathed and dressed, she stood in front of the mirror again. She was wearing the blue silk sheath she had worn for her last night out in Paris with Mandy and David, and she thought now how strange it was that outwardly she should look just the same. A little paler perhaps, but that was all. No haggard lines, no shadows round her eyes, no hint at all of the turmoil inside her. Even the bruises on her shins where she'd collided with the steel frame of the wheelchair were hidden under the sheer, tinted nylon of her tights, and as she turned to the door to go down for dinner she breathed a sigh of relief. She wouldn't even have to face Neil tonight, she thought, as she went down the stairs, and if anyone could detect a change in her it would be him. Elaine had already informed her, in rather clipped tones, that Neil was away in America at the moment, looking up some old contacts in the hope of drumming up some extra business for Brett's, and no one could deny they needed it at the moment. Since the Macmillan contract had fallen through the family firm was in dire straits, and one or two bad reports in the Press just lately hadn't helped— but no doubt tonight everyone else would be too preoccupied with the state of her grandfather's health to worry about her, and for that she was grateful.

In the hall she smoothed her palms over the blue silk and opened the door. They were all at the far end of the sitting-room, a little group round the hearth. Her mother, cool and attractive, stood in the centre, talking to James, who towered over her, a younger, more jovial edition of his father. Alexander Brett was her step-grandfather really, of course, and from this distance it could have been he who stood there; James had the same blue eyes under craggy eyebrows, the same mannerisms as his father. Only the hair was different; James's hair was still dark, if not as black as it had once been, while Alexander Brett's was a complete iron-grey. Julia was with them, lounging over one end of the sofa and sipping in a bored fashion at her glass. Only Roddy was out of the group. He was by the drinks cabinet, his cheeks already flushed, his tie loosened. He grinned across at her, his glass raised, as his eyes ran over the blue silk in open admiration. 'Hello, little sister. Last but not least, that's what I always say. What'll it be—the usual?'

Nodding, Cassie moved across to join him. 'Hello, Roddy. How are things?'

He gave a crooked grin and glanced across at his wife, who quickly looked away. 'Same as always, old love, same as always. But at least now I have a partner in crime—and a very beautiful one at that.' Bottle and glass clinked unsteadily together as he poured her sherry.

'Elaine was hopping mad over the way you skulked off after that little "contretemps" with your beloved the other week.'

'By my beloved, I assume you mean Neil?' Cassie returned sweetly, and Roddy gave her a sly look.

'Of course. Who else?'

'I would hardly say I skulked off.'

'Escaped, then?' His grin had widened and Cassie found herself grinning back. Roddy's humour was nothing less than sarcastic at the best of times, but compared to her mother's it was comic relief.

'I must say I was beginning to have grave doubts about you, little sister, very grave doubts.' He handed Cassie her drink, and for a brief moment his fingers lingered on hers. 'How about offering each other some consolation over lunch one day next week?' he suggested, and now there was something else besides humour in his face.

'You know you'll be out of town next week, Roddy,' the cool tones of Elaine Brett interposed. 'So stop embarrassing Cassie and go and be sociable to your wife. Her glass is empty.'

With a mocking bow to his mother-in-law Roddy sauntered away. Elaine watched him, her mouth tight, then turned to Cassie.

'I wish you wouldn't encourage him, Cassie. Things are difficult enough between him and Julia without complications of that sort!'

'I was merely asking him how he was, Mummy,' Cassie murmured. 'I've not seen much of him these last few months.'

Elaine looked irritated. 'He's hardly had time to stand still. James told him he had to start pulling his weight or get out—the way things are at the moment we can't afford joyriders.' She swirled the liquid in her glass, her fingers tight on the stem as she added, 'There's already been quite a few redundancies among the men.'

Cassie stared into her sherry. 'Is this what's brought on Grandfather's heart attack, do you think? Worry about the firm?'

'He's certainly been under a lot of stress lately—they both have.' Elaine looked across at James, and Cassie did the same, noticing for the first time the lines of strain around his eyes and mouth, making him look every inch his fifty years. 'The whole future of the firm is in jeopardy, Cassie, and all because of a couple of silly newspaper articles!'

'It isn't just the newspaper reports, Mummy,' Cassie returned, and her mother turned to stare at her in disbelief.

'You don't actually believe there's any truth in them, do you? That James and your grandfather would stoop to bribery and corruption to get those contracts?'

'Of course not!' Cassie replied, shifting slightly under her mother's accusing glare. 'But the whole country is in a recession. Times are hard. Brett's Engineering is bound to start feeling the pinch, just like everyone else. There's hardly a firm in the country that hasn't had to tighten their belts——'

'I'm not a fool, Cassie!' her mother snapped. 'I do read the newspapers! But that editor—Hodges, or whatever his name is—has set out to deliberately malign Brett's! Ever since Ross——' She stopped abruptly, and Cassie's eyes jerked to her mother's face again as her stomach suddenly clenched.

'Ever since Ross—what?'

'Oh—nothing!' Elaine took a final gulp of her drink, her dark eyes glittering strangely in the light from the fire as she tilted her head to catch the last few drops. Her gaze roamed restlessly round the room, before coming back to rest on Cassie again, and she added tightly, 'Believe me, Cassie, that man has a vendetta against us!'

'Who? Bill Hodges? Oh, Mummy, that's ridiculous!' Cassie tried to laugh. 'Editors don't have vendettas—they merely print what they see as the facts——'

'But he's twisting the facts to suit his own ends! He's determined to ruin Brett's Engineering!'

'But why should he want to do that?' Cassie asked, bewildered. It was unlike Elaine to get so agitated over anything, and it disturbed her. Besides, didn't Elaine know the effect her words were having? 'Bill Hodges is Ross's old editor,' she got out. 'I never met him, but Ross always spoke very highly of him...'

But Elaine seemed hardly to be listening. Her fingers were twisted round the stem of her glass, her white knuckles evidence of the pressure she was exerting. 'Just take my word for it, Cassie. That man will do anything in his power to bring us down!'

At that moment Nancy, the housekeeper, appeared, to announced that dinner was ready, and conversation was at an end as they all turned to file through into the dining-room.

James sat at the head of the table, as always, with Elaine and Roddy on his left and Julia and Cassie on his right. Only Alexander Brett's chair was empty, at the other end of the table, and Cassie stared at the empty place in faint surprise. She was guiltily aware that she had hardly given a thought to her grandfather today, so

wrapped up had she been in trying to puzzle out the
events of last night. But obviously her grandfather was
very much in the minds of her parents and Roddy, for
they spent the whole meal discussing his illness and the
effect it would have on the firm. Even Julia chimed in
occasionally, and it occurred to Cassie that she was the
only one of the family who had no need to worry about
the state of Brett's Engineering. James gave her and Julia
a more than generous allowance, but her main income
now came from the boutique, and it was there that her
financial interests lay.

Nancy brought in the pudding and the others began
murmuring together in an undertone, but Cassie was only
half aware of them. She sat silently at her end of the
table, uninterestedly prodding her pudding with her
spoon and thinking over her mother's antagonism
towards Bill Hodges. She supposed it was under-
standable, really. As James's wife, Elaine had always
aroused a certain amount of interest among the Press,
not all of which had been complimentary, and for this
reason she had never liked what she termed 'newspaper
people'. This was one of the reasons she had never got
on with Ross either, but Ross had always spoken of Bill
Hodges as a friend, as well as an editor, and the idea
was growing in Cassie's mind that she should go and see
him, find out for herself what sort of a man Bill Hodges
really was. She could talk to him about Ross, and at the
moment that was something she desperately needed to
do. Perhaps she could resolve some of these unanswered
questions that persisted in plaguing her, and after all,
what did she have to lose? He could always refuse to see
her, or, worse still, tell her to go and see a psychiatrist—
something she'd considered doing anyway.

She was half convinced she was off her head. Seeing Ross like that, so suddenly, she had almost believed it was some kind of hallucination, perhaps brought on by her nightmare the night before. But the bruises on her legs were real enough, and hallucinations didn't climb into a car and drive away into the night, leaving her standing in the rain! But then, the real Ross, the Ross she knew, wouldn't have done that either; and those grey eyes, so cold, so remote. She shivered. The way he had looked at her, almost as though he hated her. But why?

Perhaps it *would* help to talk to Bill Hodges. She certainly couldn't confide in anyone here—even her mother. She knew instinctively that Elaine would not be a sympathetic confidante. There had always been a curious kind of coldness in Elaine, a ruthlessness that somehow repelled her. Even as a child she had found it impossible to confide in her mother. Her father had been the recipient of all her childish worries, and since his disappearance from her life she had learnt to manage her own affairs.

With a sigh she pushed her dish away and looked up. Her mother was watching her, the dark eyes piercingly intent, and Cassie suddenly had the uneasy feeling that her mother could see into her mind, knew everything that was there. Then Elaine was pushing back her chair, standing up, with a sign that they should all move back into the sitting-room for coffee, and the feeling was gone.

Cassie took her coffee to the window-seat and sat with her legs curled under her, sipping slowly at her cup and staring out at the shadowy, rainwashed garden. The heavy clouds of a wet October night were glimmering strangely with the reflected glow of the city beneath them, but they were suddenly blotted out as a shadow fell across the glass and Cassie turned to see her mother standing behind her.

'You're very quiet, Cassie. Your holiday or whatever it was doesn't seem to have done you much good. Where did you get to, by the way?'

Cassie shifted along the seat as her mother made to sit next to her. 'I went to see Mandy.'

'Amanda Bradbury? The girl who went to Paris?'

'She's Amanda Newton-Smith now, Mummy, and she went to Paris with her husband. He works in the embassy there.'

Elaine stirred her coffee slowly. 'Oh, yes, I remember. His father is Sir Gerald, isn't he? She did very well for herself, marrying into that family. I only hope you have the sense to make as much of your opportunities.'

Cassie sipped at her coffee, realising with a sinking heart what her mother was alluding to. There had been no mention of her row with Neil up to now—it had been overtaken by other, more important events, but Cassie knew she would not be allowed to get away with it for long, and she was right.

'I've been thinking, Cassie,' Elaine continued. 'You're obviously not over the shock of hearing about your grandfather yet, and the few days you've had with Amanda haven't done you much good. Why don't you have a complete break for a while? Go down to the cottage for a couple of weeks; then later, when Neil gets back from his trip to New York, he can come and join you and you can have some time together——'

'I don't think that's a good idea, Mummy.'

'Why not? You always used to love going to the cottage——'

'Mummy—I think we ought to get one thing straight,' Cassie interrupted tightly. 'I'm not interested in Neil—not in *that* way, anyway.'

'And what "way" would that be?'

Cassie pressed her lips together for a moment. 'I don't love him.'

'Love?' Elaine's tinkling laugh was full of amusement. 'What a strange child you are, Cassie! You like Neil, don't you? You're fond of him? I know Neil is more than fond of you. I remember what a pet he always made of you when you were home from school——'

'It takes more than that to make a marriage, Mummy!'

'Nonsense!' Elaine stated firmly, her smile fading. 'All that is necessary is liking and respect for one's partner. In my estimation love is a very overrated emotion. It's all very well for giggling schoolgirls, but in the real world love doesn't provide a roof over your head or pay the bills!'

She picked up her cup and Cassie stared at her, unable to believe what she was hearing—even from Elaine! 'But you must have been in love at least—at least *once*?' she stammered. 'What about Daddy?'

Elaine's cup clattered into its saucer and Cassie winced at the look on her face. 'Oh, yes, I loved your father, and look where it got me—absolutely nowhere! We lived in that dingy little house in Manchester, and if I hadn't worked myself up to become personal secretary to Mr Daleford we would never have had any money for anything. And have you forgotten that awful school you used to go to? And those children you used to hang around with? At least Julia was always a little more selective with her friends!'

As Elaine bitterly recalled her first marriage, Cassie swirled the last of her coffee round her cup. Her memories of primary school had always been happy ones; it was only later that her small world had fallen apart. She could look back now with a certain amount of detachment at the bewildered eight-year-old who had clung, sobbing, to her father as he kissed her goodbye that final morning. How could she have known then that she would never see him again? That he would die so tragically, only a month after her mother's second marriage? It was only later that she had been calmly informed that Daddy didn't live with them any more—that she was to have a new Daddy—and James Brett had begun to pay regular visits to the house in Manchester. Within six months they had moved down to London, to be installed in this house, James's elegant home in a quiet, tree-lined London square, and while Elaine settled down with her new husband and Julia settled down with a new set of boyfriends, Cassie had been packed off to a suitably exclusive boarding-school for young ladies. She had hated it, but it was only after she had made herself physically ill that Elaine had relented and she had been sent to somewhere nearer home. St Hilda's wasn't exactly famous for its old girls, but at least she had settled down there and made some friends of her own. Now she swallowed the last of her coffee and set down her empty cup.

'I liked primary school, Mummy, and I can remember some of the girls I used to play with. They weren't as bad as you like to make out——'

'Well, I'll say one thing for that school, you were always top of the class!' Elaine conceded bitterly. 'But as for those girls—what did they have to look forward to? A job in a shop—or an office if they were lucky, and marriage to a man with an income not much higher than their own—if he had a job at all! At least *you* don't have to work for your living, Cassie, and you have the looks—and the opportunity—to make a decent marriage. Now, if you take my advice you'll go down to the cottage——'

'I'm not going to the cottage!' Cassie declared tightly. 'Perhaps later, yes, but tomorrow I intend going to the boutique as usual——'

'The boutique!' Elaine's tone was indicative of her feelings on that subject. 'Neil told me about your aspirations in that direction, and believe me, he won't like it——'

'Well, I'm sorry about that, but there's nothing he can do about it!' Cassie snapped, getting to her feet. The window-seat was becoming increasingly claustrophobic. 'I've already decided to accept Natalie's offer, and Neil can go to hell——'

'Cassandra!'

'What on earth are you hassling Cassie about now, Elaine?' James Brett's deep tones interrupted Elaine's furious exclamation, and Cassie turned to her stepfather in relief. 'The child's been in bed all day and here you are giving her the third degree!'

'James, you don't understand——' Elaine also rose to meet her husband. 'I've tried to talk Cassie into going to the cottage for a few days, but she insists on going into the boutique tomorrow!'

James raised an eyebrow, his mouth quirking into a rueful grin. 'Well, I can't say I blame her. I always had to be prised away from my desk——'

'But, James——' Elaine persisted, her hand on his arm. 'Cassie is going to accept Natalie Peers' offer of a partnership in that fashion business, and you know how unstable——'

'Is she now?' James was suddenly alert, his attention immediately riveted. 'Neil tells me you've got quite a head for business, young lady. It looks as though some of the Brett business acumen has rubbed off on you, at least. Tell me, what are Miss Peers' terms? I take it she is asking you to invest a lump sum?'

Thankfully Cassie began to discuss the details of Natalie's proposition with her stepfather, and Elaine sank back on to the window-seat with a hiss of frustration. She was furious, Cassie knew, at being thwarted in this way, but Cassie also knew that she would never cause a scene in front of James.

As luck would have it, Julia claimed her mother's attention after that, and at ten o'clock Cassie decided she had had enough. She excused herself on the grounds that she had a headache and escaped thankfully up to bed. Her excuse was real enough; there was a painful throbbing behind her eyes—brought on by the knowledge that her mother was doing everything she could to manoeuvre her into a suitable marriage with Neil.

Bill Hodges was a swarthy, thick-set man in a waistcoat and a creased pink shirt. Cassie advanced into his cluttered office and held out her hand. 'Mr Hodges?'

But his own hands remained firmly in his waistcoat pockets as he swivelled slowly in his chair, appraising her narrowly from under bushy black brows. 'And you are Cassandra Beresford—James Brett's stepdaughter. You've had a wasted journey, Miss Beresford. If he's sent you to plead his case you're wasting your time. Now, if you'll excuse me, I'm a very busy man...'

Cassie stared at him, stunned into silence. This wasn't at all what she'd expected. It was almost a week now since she'd first decided to see him, and despite her initial determination she'd spent all this morning wondering whether or not she was doing the right thing in coming here. She'd been to see her grandfather twice now, and, although she had been deeply shocked at the sight of the once powerful frame lying useless and immobile in a hospital bed, there had been no more disturbing encounters in the dimly lit corridors, and she was beginning to think that maybe she *had* had some kind of hallucination after all, perhaps brought on by her nightmare the night before. As the week had progressed and she'd become immersed in the day-to-day routine of work again, her reasons for making this appointment, reasons that had seemed so desperately important on Sunday evening, had begun to seem less and less so, and even Natalie, when she'd learned who it was she was coming to see, had tried to dissuade her, insisting she was simply raking up more pain for herself by coming here.

But still, here she was, even though all she could think about on the way up here was—what was she going to say? And how would she say it? And now that she was actually in here, this odious little man was trying to pack her off without a word! Suddenly temper was burning inside her with a furious flame.

'I won't take up much of your time, Mr Hodges,' she declared tightly. 'And despite what you think, it's not those libellous articles on Brett's Engineering that I wanted to see you about—I leave all that sort of thing to my stepfather's solicitors!' she added coldly. 'My business is more of a—a personal nature.'

Bill Hodges picked up his pen and began to study the papers in front of him. 'Then I suggest you write to our agony aunt, "Dear Daisy". She's more qualified to deal with that kind of thing than I am.'

Cassie glared at him. 'It's about Ross Tyler,' she declared baldly. 'I believe you were a friend of his—as well as his editor.'

Bill Hodges threw down his pen and sat back in his chair again. 'What about Ross?'

There had been no change in his features, but Cassie sensed a slight change of attitude. She shifted slightly, before continuing more slowly, 'Well, I—I knew Ross—personally. We were going to be married.'

There was a silence. Bill Hodges stared at her for a moment, then with an exclamation he swung himself out of his chair to pace to the window and stare out. After a moment he turned to her again. 'My God, so *you* were the girl . . . ?'

Cassie nodded. 'I was in the car with him when he crashed,' she supplied tonelessly.

Bill Hodges ran his fingers through already ruffled black hair. 'So *that's* it! I should have known there was more to those bloody features than he was letting on; he was almost *obsessed* . . .'

He was frowning out of the window again, and Cassie stared uncomprehendingly at his back. He seemed to have forgotten she was there. 'I'm sorry, I don't understand——' she began. 'Who was obsessed?'

He turned then and moved back to the desk. 'Ross always was a damned good journalist, but he put a hell of a lot into those features—too much! I should have *guessed* there was something . . .' He banged his fist down on the desk, making the telephone ting faintly, but Cassie could only stare at him, her whole body suddenly taut.

'You mean—*Ross* wrote those articles about Brett's Engineering?'

'Of course—who else? He was working on them before his accident. He'd always had a bit of a thing about Brett's, ever since some old guy he knew up in Manchester went out of business a few years ago. There was some shady dealing involving Brett's——'

'Mr Hodges, if this is another of your libellous accusations——' Cassie interrupted tightly, but he held up his hands.

'Believe me, lady, this came from Ross himself. The old man's name was Nick something-or-other——'

'Not his *Uncle* Nick?' Cassie exclaimed, her eyes jerking back to Bill Hodges' face.

'Ross never said anything about the guy being his uncle, simply that he was some distant relative of his father's——'

'Yes—yes, he was,' Cassie interrupted faintly. 'Ross's parents died when he was small and he was in foster homes until his Uncle Nick took him in.' She felt as though she needed to sit down, but the nearest chair was out of reach so she stayed where she was, leaning weakly against a filing cabinet.

'You knew him?' Bill Hodges questioned sharply.

'No, no, I never met him, and Ross never talked about him much, except to tell me that he lived in Cumbria or somewhere——'

'Lancashire,' Bill Hodges corrected her, 'and by God, if this is true, Ross has a hell of a lot to answer for——' He sat down behind the desk again, ruffling his fingers through his hair.

'But—what does all this have to do with Brett's?' Cassie asked dazedly.

'The old man was an engineer,' Bill Hodges began abruptly. 'Brilliant, by all accounts. He had a firm in Manchester. They put in a tender for a new office block or something; anyway, the long and the short of it is, the designs disappeared, with the result that Brett's got the contract—with an almost identical design. Of course, there was an inquiry and nothing was ever proved, but when we decided to do a series on British engineering, Ross begged for the job. He told me he had inside information—and certainly he knew his stuff. He soon got wind of what sounded like double dealing in the ranks at Brett's, but then I didn't realise just how "inside" his information really was. But you must have known something about this?' He was watching Cassie through narrowed eyes.

'No—no, I had no idea,' Cassie got out. And then, 'But—but why have you waited so long? To publish the articles, I mean? Surely if Ross wrote them——'

'Miss Beresford,' Bill Hodges interrupted tersely, 'this is a newspaper, not a women's glossy magazine! We print our stuff as we get it, whether it's front-page news or— my God!'

In a second he was round the desk and had produced a chair for her to collapse into as her legs finally gave way beneath her.

'As—as you get it?' she echoed faintly. 'But—but that's impossible! Ross is *dead*!'

'*Dead?* God, if he is it'd make a hell of a story!'

'But—the accident—there was no time——' she stammered incoherently.

'Sure, Ross was in a bad way. His legs were pretty badly smashed up, he was unconscious for a couple of days. I believe the driver's side of the car took the full force of the smash—but believe me, lady, it'd take a lot more than a car smash to finish Ross Tyler. He's as alive as you or I, and I'd give a hell of a lot to know who told you otherwise!'

CHAPTER TWO

WITH A hiss of impatience Cassie stopped the car and peered out through the streaming windscreen. The narrow, twisting road disappeared in front of her round yet another blind corner, and the mist-shrouded hills which rose steeply on either side of the road were rapidly disappearing into the gathering darkness. She was lost— she'd obviously taken a wrong turning somewhere, and there wasn't a house, or a farm, or any sign of human habitation anywhere that she could see.

Reluctantly she pulled the hood of her coat up and climbed out into the rain, to stand by the car and peer back along the way she had come. The road had been climbing steadily for the last half-hour, but as far as she could see it only took her into yet another fold of these vast, brooding hills, probably ending in yet another farm track.

She'd forgotten how remote, how alien this northernmost corner of Lancashire could be. The Pennines seemed to close in on her like watchful giants, and she shivered as she thrust her hands into the warm pockets of her coat and searched the hills yet again for a farmhouse, a glimmer of light, anything that she could make for to ask directions. It was cold, too, much colder than it had been in Birmingham where she'd stopped for lunch, and there was the sound of water everywhere. The rain was falling steadily on grass and leaves, beating a tattoo on the roof of the car and running along the surface of the road, forming little streams, or becks, as she knew they were called in these parts, which ran for a little way then disappeared again into fields and roadside drains.

It had been raining steadily since she had left the motorway at Preston to join the A6, eventually turning off yet again to climb into these wild, lonely hills. And she didn't even know what she was looking for! All she had was a crumpled piece of paper—Bill Hodges had given her Ross's address only after much persuasion on her part—and after what seemed now like a crazy impulse she had determined to come up here this weekend and try to see Ross for herself, to try and sort out the whys and wherefores of this whole crazy situation.

So here she was, stuck on a hillside, without a hope in hell of finding anything before darkness descended! And if she didn't get a move on she'd be stuck on the hill all night—the thought of which made her shiver yet again and glance over her shoulder at the dark mass rising behind her. Looking quickly up and down the road, she decided it was too narrow to turn here; she would have to carry on until she found a place to turn and then she would go back to the cluster of cottages— it could hardly be called a village—that she'd passed through some miles back. Perhaps there she would find someone to give her directions, and she would head for the nearest hotel and book a meal and a room for the night. She could review her situation in the morning; there was no point in driving along these narrow lanes in the dark, and besides, the rain seemed to be getting even heavier, if that were possible!

Her mind made up, Cassie climbed back into the car and set off again, more slowly this time, headlights on main beam as she searched the narrow verges, looking for a gate or some break in the endless dry stone walls where she could turn the Metro.

At last she came to what looked like a farm gateway. Two tall stone pillars guarded a cattle grid and a rough track disappeared into the wet darkness. With a murmur of relief she put the Metro into reverse and backed into the gateway—only to give a cry of alarm as the car suddenly lurched violently and there was a terrific, nerve-grinding crunch.

With a shudder the engine died, and Cassie scrambled out into the rain again, her stomach tied in knots at the thought of what she might find.

There was a ditch on the far side of the wall, impossible to see from the road, with a torrent of rainwater burbling and gurgling its way along the stony bottom, disappearing into a drain under the cattle grid and reappearing on the other side to continue its way down the hill. She had obviously reversed just a little too far, and the offside rear wheel of the car had slid down into the ditch, dragging the car half off the cattle grid and wedging it against one of the stone pillars.

Without a thought for her suede boots, she stepped off the cattle grid and squelched round to the back of the car to see what could be done. The hot exhaust was hissing and sending up a trail of steam whenever it came into contact with the icy water of the beck, but she ignored this and put her shoulder against the rear window to give a tentative heave. Nothing happened—except that her arm ached and her boots slipped in the quagmire of grass and mud. After a moment of helpless anger she squelched round to the driver's side again to scrabble under the dashboard for the torch. This time she went round to the front to see what could be done from that side, but, if anything, it looked worse, and as the beam from the torch glinted on bare metal she gave a despairing thought to what it was going to cost her to have the damage repaired.

She switched the torch off and looked frustratedly up and down the road, then up the now only faintly discernible cart track, and as her eyes scanned the dark hillside she thought she glimpsed a faint light. She looked again, searching carefully. There was definitely a light up there, but what it was and how far away she couldn't tell. However, there was nothing else for it, and after switching the car lights off and locking the doors—a precaution she hardly thought was necessary under the circumstances—she set off up the track with the light from the torch for guidance.

She had to pick her way along the track. What wasn't covered in enormous puddles was rough and uneven, causing her to stumble a couple of times, but at least the light she had glimpsed earlier was getting closer, and after a few minutes she realised what it was—the dim glow of heavy curtains drawn across a lighted window.

The sound of the rain had altered, and she knew there were trees somewhere close. The track veered round, and suddenly she was walking on gravel, a level drive which swept round to the dark shape of a rambling, stone-built house. There were lights in at least two ground-floor windows that she could see, and she quickened her pace to stumble up the steps and hammer on the front door.

It seemed an age before a light over the door flicked on, making her blink, and the heavy door swung back to reveal a tall, square-faced man with wiry, greying hair, formally dressed in a dark suit and tie.

He stared out at her, stony-faced, and Cassie burst into a stammered explanation, feeling daunted somehow by that dark suit. It seemed strangely incongruous in this wild, lonely place.

'I—I'm sorry to bother you, but I've had an accident, and my car's blocking your gate. Have—have you got a tractor or—or something to give me a tow? Or a phone—so that I could phone a garage?'

'There are no garages here, miss. At least, none that will come up here at this time of night.'

'A tractor, then?' she asked, trying to keep the tremor out of her voice, but his eyebrows rose chillingly.

'This is not a farm, miss!'

'I—I realise that, but the car is well and truly stuck in a ditch. I was trying to turn...' She gazed up at him helplessly, but the stony face remained unmoved, and it suddenly occurred to her that he could be wondering what she was doing wandering round the hills in the dark.

'I'm looking for a house,' she added, by way of explanation. 'The Breck. Do you know it?'

Now she knew she had a response, for his eyebrows rose even further as he surveyed her from head to foot. '*This* is The Breck, miss. May I know the nature of your business?'

'This—*this* is The Breck?' she stammered, stunned, then began again, hurriedly, 'I'm looking for Ross—Mr Ross Tyler—is he here?' Overwhelming relief and anticipation made her step up to the top step, but he remained where he was, a solid wall, and she hurriedly stepped down again. 'My name is Cassie—Cassandra Beresford.'

'Step this way please, miss.'

She was finally allowed inside, where a pointed glance at her muddy boots had her hurriedly wiping her feet on the mat. The heavy door was swung to and she was led across a darkly panelled hall and through another door, with instructions to, 'Wait here a moment, please, miss.'

She was in a lamplit study, comfortably furnished, with a huge desk in one corner, flanked by rows of book-shelves, and a deep, wing-backed armchair set in front of a blazing fire. She moved across to stand on the thick hearthrug and stretch her hands out to the blaze, feeling some of the tension of the last half-hour begin to melt away as warmth seeped painfully back to her frozen limbs and other feelings, far more potent, began to grip her. Excitement, anticipation, fear...

She looked up and caught sight of herself in the mirror over the hearth, grimacing at the picture she presented. No wonder his lordship with the suit had been reluctant to let her in! Her hair was plastered to her forehead and her cheeks and nose were bright red with cold, as well as bearing the occasional muddy smear. The shoulders of her coat were darkly wet with rain, and she looked down to find that the rest of her coat had fared no better. There was mud there also, where she'd leant against the car, and her boots were probably beyond all hope. Pulling out her handkerchief to wipe the mud off her cheeks, she looked into the mirror again—and froze in shock. Grey eyes met hers. Ross stood at the other end of the room, his back against the door, watching her.

She swung round, and it flashed through her mind in that first split second that he was not surprised to see her, but this thought was pushed away as she took in the long, lean length of him, and her eyes widened in a dazed surprise.

She had expected, at the very least, that he would be in a wheelchair, as he had been at the hospital this time last week. But he was on his feet, albeit leaning heavily on two sticks, and looking darkly attractive in a black velvet dinner-jacket and white frilled shirt.

He was thinner, leaner than she remembered, and there were lines deeply etched from cheek to jaw which hadn't been there before, giving him a bitter, almost cynical appearance. His mouth, too, had a grim twist to it, and the grey eyes were hard and unyielding. He was the same, yet so very, very different, and her heart contracted at the pain she could see etched into every line of his face.

'Ross,' she breathed, and in a second she was across the room, sliding her arms round his waist, pressing herself against him with all the pent-up longing of the last eighteen months. A wave of emotion was suddenly making it difficult to breathe. 'Oh, Ross——' she choked. 'I thought you were dead!' And as the tears welled and overflowed, sliding unchecked down her cheeks, she pressed her face into his neck, savouring the warmth of his body, the familiar masculine smell of him, the feel of his skin, damp with the salty tang of her tears, against her lips. It was ecstasy to hold him like this, sheer joy just to be with him again.

'No doubt you would have preferred it if I were dead,' he said, and she was suddenly still.

She looked up, registering for the first time that his body was hard and tense under her fingers, as though he was holding himself rigidly in check, and it dawned on her too that he had made no move to put his arms round her, or hold her to him in any way—in fact, he hadn't moved a muscle since she had run to him. His face, too, was rigid, and slowly she began to draw away from the taut features, the two slits of grey ice which were his eyes.

Her bewilderment must have shown in her face, for his mouth twisted. 'By God, you're good, I'll give you that. Even down to the bloody tears!'

Icy fingers began to clench in her stomach and slide up to clutch at her heart. 'Ross—don't!' she whispered. 'Please don't say things like that——'

'Why not? Doesn't it fit in with your little game? Perhaps I should have been waiting with open arms, ready to welcome you back into my life? No doubt you would have preferred that! Then you could smile and tell me how much you've missed me, that it was all some kind of ghastly mistake——'

His voice had her flinching away from him, and the smile he gave was completely without humour.

'My God, if I didn't know better you'd have me totally convinced!'

She couldn't speak for the tightness in her throat, could only stare at him, and he continued in that same, coldly expressionless voice, 'It might have been interesting to see just how far you were willing to go in this little charade—or were you prepared to give your all to save Brett's Engineering? Either way, you took a hell of a risk coming here.'

'I—I don't understand...'

'Oh, come off it, Cassie,' he bit out. 'That wide-eyed innocent act may have worked with me once, but I'm damned if I'll fall for it again. Things must be pretty desperate at Brett's for McAllister to allow his future wife to sacrifice herself for the sake of the firm!' He turned away, towards the desk, manoeuvring himself on the sticks to reach down and open a drawer, pulling out a bottle of whisky, then a glass.

'His future wife——?' she echoed, staring at him, and a small ray of hope leapt inside her. Was *that* what all this was about? Was Ross jealous? Did he, too, assume that she was going to marry Neil? 'Ross——' she began quickly, 'Ross, it's not what you think! I never meant to marry Neil——'

He threw her a swift, all-encompassing glance. 'Deserting the sinking ship, eh? I can almost feel sorry for the poor bastard!'

He poured himself a generous measure of spirit into the glass and she watched him as if in a daze. The contempt in his eyes filled her with dreadful fear, a terrible weight pressing down on her heart, making it almost impossible for her to think, or move, or speak, but she needed desperately to think, to try to explain...

There was a tap on the door and the man with the suit entered, only now he was wearing a thick waterproof jacket over his suit, and carrying a flashlight.

Ross took a gulp of his whisky before turning to him. 'Well?'

The other man nodded. 'It's as the young lady says, Mr Ross. The car's in the ditch by the old gate.'

'Can you get it out?'

'I'll have a go, but it's wrapped round the gatepost—in a right mess!'

'OK, Willis. Thanks.'

The man nodded and went out, without so much as a flicker in Cassie's direction, and Ross stared into his whisky.

'You needn't have gone to all that trouble, Cassie. In fact, you could have saved yourself a journey. Bill Hodges doesn't like his journalists being "emotionally involved". After your little visit to his office he's refused to accept any more articles on Brett's Engineering.'

Cassie was still staring at him. 'You really don't believe me, do you?' she asked faintly, and her voice didn't sound like her voice at all. 'You think I've come about those articles—but you don't understand. I'm trying to tell you—I thought you were dead!'

She waited for him to look up, to smile at her, to open his arms to her—but he was still staring into his whisky.

There was a silence, and then he said flatly, 'Am I supposed to say something to that?'

She felt as though he'd dealt her a physical blow. This was some horrible kind of joke—it had to be! She moved forward, facing him across the desk, bringing her hands down on to its leather topped surface as though she needed desperately to hold on to something solid.

'Do you really think I'd set all this up—trail all the way up here—just to stop you writing those articles?' she got out.

'Oh, no, not just to stop me writing those articles. There's far more to it than that now, isn't there, Cassie? There's the small question of some missing designs, for one thing.'

She stared at him. 'Your Uncle Nick,' she intoned hollowly. And now she could no longer deny the fear that was inside her, that had been inside her ever since her interview with Bill Hodges. She had buried it deep down, refusing even to acknowledge it, but now it was growing, expanding, threatening to overwhelm her completely...

'At least you're not going to try and tell me you know nothing about *that*!' Ross murmured, a grim twist to his mouth, and she swallowed painfully.

'Bill Hodges told me.'

His eyebrows rose, coolly questioning. 'Bill Hodges? Are you sure it wasn't your stepfather? Or your grandfather—the great Sir Alexander Brett himself?'

'My grandfather's in hospital,' she whispered. 'He nearly died last weekend.'

'So that was why you were at the hospital,' he bit out. 'I did wonder. No doubt you nearly died yourself when you saw me!'

'I thought I was having hallucinations,' she said faintly, remembering the trauma of those few brief seconds. 'I thought I'd seen a ghost——'

'No doubt you thought, too, just how much of a threat I could still be to your precious family firm!' He raised his glass to his lips, draining the last of his whisky in one quick gulp. 'Tell me, Cassie, is that why you were sent up here? To see what could be salvaged from Brett's declining reputation?'

Her eyes had focused on him again. 'Why won't you understand? These last months—*I thought you were dead*! Do you really believe I'd have stayed away all this time if I'd known you were alive—living here? Injured?' Her eyes flickered over the sticks.

He looked up then, and she shrank away, drymouthed, from what she could see in his eyes.

'Injured? What's the matter, Cassie? Can't you bring yourself to say *crippled*?' He brought his fist down on the desktop, almost smashing the glass in his hand, and his mouth twisted as he continued, deadly soft, 'I would never have believed it of you, Cassie, not of *you*, but by God, you're no better than the rest of them! You walked out on me. You thought I was going to die— that I was no longer a threat to Brett's Engineering—so you simply turned your back and walked away without so much as a second glance! It took me four weeks, Cassie, four bloody, agonising weeks, and then I *had* to believe it. I came to my senses then. I swore I'd make you pay, and by God, I will, Cassie. I'll destroy you the way you tried to destroy me. I'll bring Brett's to its knees in any way I can. You may have stopped me writing those articles but there's plenty more I can do yet, *plenty* more!'

Cassie stood rooted to the spot, shocked beyond belief by those bitter, burning eyes and that twisted mouth. The world seemed to be collapsing round her and there was a tightness, a pain around her heart that would not be shaken off, but she faced him, her eyes wide and darkly green, realising, as if for the first time, that she had never really known this man before. He was a stranger to her, he wasn't the Ross she had loved and lost and wept for all these long lonely months. He was a man twisted by pain and bitterness, concerned only with the wrongs he thought had been done to him, and his own selfish need for revenge. She straightened slowly from the desk, drawing herself up, gathering her shattered emotions round her like a cloak. She took a step towards the door, but he was in front of her, blocking the way.

'Well?' he bit out. 'Have you nothing to say? No tears of denial?'

She turned those huge eyes on him again. 'I loved you,' she whispered through stiff lips. 'I loved you, Ross, but you never loved me, did you? I was just Alex Brett's granddaughter to you, and yet every day since that damned accident I've died for you in my heart. I've spent the last eighteen months pining for a man who didn't give a damn!'

She turned to the door again, but his hand shot out and grabbed her wrist. 'Cassie!' he grated, but she flinched away, trying to wrench herself out of his grasp. Anger was burning inside her now, furious, bitter anger, and she welcomed it, clasped its heat to her to ward away the deathly chill that was in her heart.

'By God!' she blazed at him. 'How can you stand there and accuse me of deserting you—when it was you who deserted me? You used me, Ross. You used me for everything you could get! Names—addresses—information—that was all you wanted, wasn't it? Tell me, would you have carried it through, Ross? Did you ever *really* intend to marry me?'

'Damn you, Cassie!' he grated. 'I should have come after you then, as I wanted to—then we would have seen who was using who——'

'Then why didn't you?' she cried. 'You left me all this time believing you were dead! You left me to suffer——'

'*I couldn't walk!*' he interrupted fiercely. 'I couldn't even sit up in bed!'

'And so you planned all this as some kind of revenge?' she choked. 'To avenge your uncle—to avenge yourself? My God—I don't understand any of it—I don't understand *you*! If this is some kind of cruel joke, then I think you're sick—*sick*——!'

'*Excuse me.*'

Cassie's increasingly hysterical tirade was brought to an abrupt halt by the sound of a woman's voice, and they both turned as one towards the figure by the door. So intent had they been on each other that neither of them had even heard the door open.

'Ross, darling, your coffee is getting cold,' the newcomer announced in a soft drawl. 'Will you be long?'

Her eyes drifted down over Cassie as she spoke, and Cassie stared back, blankly at first, and then slowly beginning to register the slender elegance, the exquisitely made-up face, the dark eyes which, even as she watched, switched back to Ross and melted in a smilingly subtle invitation.

'Give me a moment, Elise,' Ross snapped. 'Willis will get you anything you need.' He was frowning impatiently at the interruption, and after only a brief glance at the woman by the door his dark, furious gaze was fixed on Cassie again.

The woman's eyebrows rose in silent comment, but she withdrew obediently, closing the door behind her, and Cassie turned back to Ross, her eyes brilliant now with accusation.

He had a woman here, a *woman*! The pain around her heart was now a steel band across her chest, but she managed to wrench her wrist out of his grasp.

'You—you bastard!' she choked, and headed blindly for the door, but his harsh 'Cassandra!' brought her to a halt.

'Where the hell do you think you're going?'

'Anywhere that's away from here,' she got out unsteadily.

'And how are you going to get "anywhere" with your car in the ditch?'

His clipped words brought the sudden realisation of her own predicament, but she turned to face him, head up. 'I've got legs. I'll walk.'

His furious features seemed to darken even more. 'The nearest house is three miles away, across the hill, and those boots weren't designed for fell-walking.' His scathing glance flicked to her boots and back.

'I'm not staying here,' she choked. 'I'd rather sleep in a ditch——'

'Don't be a fool!' he bit out roughly. *'Willis!'*

Willis appeared once more, coolly aloof in the dark suit, and Cassie backed away.

'I'm not staying here!' she repeated, panicking, and had to quell the urge to push her way past Willis and race out into the night. Hysterics would get her nowhere, she told herself fiercely, and yet never before had she felt the urge to scream and kick and bite as she did now, anything to get away from this dark, menacing stranger with his glittering eyes, who was advancing on her relentlessly. Taking a breath, she stood her ground, flinching as Ross's fingers fastened painfully round her arm once more.

'You're staying here!' he muttered through his teeth. 'I'm not having you wandering round the hills in the dark and making my neighbours wonder what in God's name I've been doing to you! Besides—dying of pneumonia would be too easy! Now, go and get out of those wet things.'

The look he gave her made her tremble, but still she stood her ground, facing him mutely, and with an exclamation he thrust her towards Willis.

'Get Dora to see to her!' he ordered abruptly. 'And tell her not to take her eyes off her until she's out of those wet things and in a warm bath. No doubt Mrs Maxwell will have a spare nightdress, and when she's had something to eat put her to bed!' He turned towards the desk, reaching for the whisky again. 'And Cassie——'

She turned, quivering with resentment and humiliation and painful desolation, to stare at his back.

'You can give Willis your car keys and take your boots off in the hall before you go up, and, so you don't get any ideas——' he turned slowly to face her again, his eyes dangerously mocking '—if you give Willis any trouble then you'll sleep in the dressing-room that adjoins my room. Understand?'

She stared at him, and as comprehension dawned her eyes blazed. His mouth twisted in grim amusement, but before she could think up a suitable retort Willis had taken her arm and was leading her firmly out of the door.

CHAPTER THREE

DORA was presumably Willis's wife, although Cassie would never have guessed it from her appearance, Dora being small and round to Willis's sparse length. Unlike Willis, Dora's dark eyes were fixed on Cassie in frank appraisal; but if she wondered why this girl who had appeared out of nowhere should receive such a volcanic reception from the master of the house she kept her questions to herself, keeping her mouth compressed into a firm line as Cassie silently handed her first the sodden coat, then her damp dress and slip.

And Cassie was glad of her silence; she was in no mood to talk. In fact she was only half aware of the other woman. Her head was full of the scene with Ross. Pictures were flashing across her mind like scenes from a film, and, like a film, she felt strangely detached from it all, as though she was a spectator, interested in the outcome, but not emotionally involved. Even the pain seemed less intense, and now she felt only a kind of desolate emptiness, but she told herself wearily that it didn't matter. None of this mattered. The only important thing now was that she should get away from here as soon as possible. She would go home tomorrow and never come anywhere remotely near this place again.

Dora collected up the wet things and bustled out, and Cassie shut herself in the steamy isolation of the bathroom. She climbed into the bath and lay back against the fragrant bubbles, closing her eyes. The water was warm, a soothing balm against the taut muscles of her cold body, but she hardly felt it. Only when Dora had rapped on the door for the second time, to enquire if she had everything she needed, did she rouse herself sufficiently to begin soaping herself.

She finally emerged into the bedroom again, still rubbing her damp hair, to find a delicate lacy nightdress draped across the bed. She stared at it uncomprehendingly for a moment, then snatched it up and flung it into a corner, breathing hard and deriving a certain amount of satisfaction from such a childishly emotional display. *Damn Ross,* she screamed silently. *Damn him!* She would not wear anything belonging to the woman called Elise. Her own underwear would have to do.

She didn't remember sleeping at all that night, but she must finally have fallen into a kind of doze, for the next thing she knew it was daylight and Dora had appeared again, this time with a tray. She struggled to sit up, blinking dazedly, as Dora placed the tray across her knees and moved round to tug the bedcovers into some semblance of order.

'It's a fine, bright morning,' Dora announced, as she drew the curtains back. Then she turned, hands on hips, to survey the bed and its occupant. 'Willis brought your case up from your car, miss, and your other things will be ready later.' She paused, surveying Cassie thoughtfully. 'I reckoned as how you might prefer to have your breakfast up here this morning.'

There was a wealth of meaning behind her words, and the corners of Cassie's mouth lifted in a travesty of a smile.

'Thank you,' she murmured. She certainly couldn't face the thought of seeing Ross again just yet.

Dora nodded, apparently satisfied, and after another quick tug at the curtains left Cassie to her breakfast.

Cassie stared at the food. She hadn't eaten anything since yesterday lunch time, having been unable to eat any of the supper Dora had set out for her last night. The steel band that closed round her heart whenever she thought of the scene with Ross had made it almost impossible for her to swallow anything, and when she had managed to force something past the tightness in her throat she had felt almost physically sick. But now her stomach was reacting noisily, and at least the food would fortify her in some measure for whatever today had to bring, she thought unhappily.

It was the thought of getting away from here that was spurring her on, but Cassie was washed and dressed in cord jeans and a thick sweater before she realised she had nothing for her feet. Willis had brought her case up, but left the spare pair of shoes she'd brought with her in the boot of the car. And as for her boots—even if they were wearable, she hadn't a clue where they were. Frowning at herself in the mirror, she pulled the brush through her hair, then picked up the tray and slipped quietly out on to the landing.

Her bare feet made hardly any sound on the stair carpet. The house was quiet, darkly silent, but a glance at her watch told her it was well past ten o'clock—much later than she'd thought. She halted uncertainly in the hall for a moment, listening, while her eyes ran over the dark wood panelling, the heavy, polished oak chest set against the far wall, and a beautifully arranged vase of roses on the small telephone table. Four doors led off from the hall. One, she knew from last evening, led to the study. One of the others, she guessed, would be the dining-room. That left two. Taking a chance, she went through the farthest door and found herself in a narrow passage, which in turn led to a large, bright kitchen. To her surprise there were modern kitchen units and worktops, with a huge red Aga set into the shell of the old fireplace. Copper pans glinted against the dark beams of the old ceiling, and in the centre of the kitchen Dora was busily rolling out pastry on a table, humming tunelessly to herself all the while.

She looked up at Cassie's entrance, and with an exclamation came forward to take the tray. 'You needn't have bothered with the tray, miss,' she clucked reprovingly, and went to set it down by the sink. Cassie followed more slowly, her toes curling on the cold, tiled floor.

'Have you any idea where my boots are?' she asked, looking round, and Dora threw a glance over her shoulder at Cassie's bare feet.

'You'll be wanting to go outside, miss?'

'I want to see about my car,' Cassie returned determinedly. 'I'm hoping to be well on my way by lunch time.'

Dora gave her a strange look but made no comment, merely nodding towards the kitchen door which stood wide open to the morning sunlight. 'Your boots'll not be fit for wearing yet, miss, but there's some wellies by the door. You're welcome to try a pair; the yard's awful mucky after all the rain we've had this last week.'

There was a small porch built over the kitchen door, no doubt to protect it from the worst of the weather, with several pairs of wellingtons lined up by the outer door, all looking equally muddy and well used. There was no indication of who each pair belonged to, and, pushing away the thought of what Ross might say if he caught her wearing *his* wellingtons, she set off across the yard. The wellingtons were too big, but they were dry, and that was all that mattered, she told herself firmly.

As Dora had said, it was a fine morning. The rain had cleared, leaving a few faint wisps of cloud hanging delicately across the clear blue of the sky. Cassie breathed in the clear Pennine air and shaded her eyes to stand and stare at the green and gold and brown of the bracken-covered hills. Nearer to hand the fields were shimmering with gossamer, silky down that swaddled the new-washed grass and danced gently in the breeze.

In other circumstances it would have been wonderful to spend a few days up here, walking the hills, as she had done years ago with her father.

It had been a favourite haunt for a day out at weekend. They would drive up in her father's old Morris, through the Trough of Bowland, and find a quiet spot to park the car. Then, while her mother and Julia listened to the radio, Cassie and her father would set off for a leisurely ramble, or scramble up to the nearest vantage point and sit for a while, just looking. Then they would make their way back to the car for a picnic tea before heading back the way they had come, through the darkening hills to the city lights of Manchester.

She had always treasured the memory of those days out with her father. It was strange that she should return to almost the very same hills in search of other, stronger memories... She brought her thoughts to an abrupt halt, thrusting her hands into the pockets of her jeans and setting off briskly down the gravel drive, towards the road.

The drive was obviously newly laid. It curved gracefully round the hill before sweeping down to the road,
to which access was barred by an impressive gateway.
The track Cassie had come up last night was obviously
the old entrance; much closer to the house but up a steep,
rocky incline, deeply rutted from years of use, and
looking just as rough in daylight as it had done last night
by the light of her torch.

If all the old drive had been as bad as this, no wonder
a new drive had been laid, Cassie thought, as she picked
her way across a mire of squelchy mud. Probably this
track would have been almost impassable to vehicles in
winter, cutting the house off completely from what few
neighbours it had.

She made her way steadily downwards towards the
road, keeping her eyes on the track but glancing up every
now and then to look further ahead, searching for the
place where the track joined the road and shading her
eyes for a glimpse of the blue Metro. But when the road
came into view she stopped in her tracks, staring. The
car had gone.

She turned to look back up the track towards the
house, and then back to the road again, before continuing down the track to walk out into the road and
look up and down, frowning in puzzlement. For a
moment she wondered if she was in the right place, but
there were the two stone gateposts and the cattle grid,
with the beck burbling along behind the wall, and there
was a scratch of blue paint on one of the gateposts, where
the car had scraped against it. This was the place—but
where was the car? She began to walk slowly back up
the track towards the house.

The house was typical of many in this part of Britain. Stone-built, solid, with a stand of trees to protect it from the worst of the weather. There was a stretch of lawn at the front, bordered by rhododendrons, which in turn gave on to a forestry plantation, with rows of conifers marching away across the hill, like a regiment of soldiers lined up before their general.

The murmuring trees were a fitting backdrop for the house, somehow softening the edges, mellowing the stone, and the vivid autumn red of the virginia creeper that trailed across the front added to this effect, enhancing the timeless beauty of the place. No wonder Ross had always spoken of it as home.

He'd never talked much about his past, and she wondered now if there was anything else he had deliberately kept hidden from her. But then, nothing could be as bad as what she knew already—could it? The fact that he had deliberately deceived her—it was still too painful to think about.

Even the house wasn't what she expected. It was much larger than she'd imagined, and with a certain faded charm, although from the look of things Ross was in the process of renovating it—there was a cement mixer and piles of bricks by the entrance to the yard.

Presumably the old man was dead now. She remember Ross telling her once that eventually the house would come to him. He had talked of giving up his job in London, of moving up here permanently, that this would be a marvellous place to bring up children...

A low stone wall swept round to some outbuildings tucked away behind the house and Cassie followed it round, determinedly dragging her thoughts back to the present. She didn't want to think of that, she didn't want to think of anything except getting away from this place. Getting away from Ross.

She rounded the corner of the house and came to a sudden halt. Ross himself stood in the middle of the cobbled yard, watching her, and from his expression it was obvious that he knew where she had been, and why.

He was casually dressed this morning in jeans, a thick shirt and leather jerkin, but even in the faded denims, and leaning heavily on the sticks, he still exuded an aura of dangerous masculinity that made Cassie's heart begin to pound painfully against her ribs.

Slowly she advanced into the yard, and one dark eyebrow quirked upwards.

'Looking for something?' he drawled.

She swallowed. 'My car. Where is it?'

His glance swept down the length of her, taking in her jumper and jeans, and lastly, the wellingtons. His mouth compressed.

'You took my boots,' she reminded him tightly. 'Dora said I could wear these.'

'Well, I won't need them now, will I?' he bit out, and she felt herself flushing uncomfortably.

'Where is my car?' she repeated unsteadily.

His eyes came back up to her face again, narrowing on her golden hair, blown into wild disorder by the wind, her eyes, wide and green, and her cheeks, pink now in spite of herself under that piercing scrutiny, but she refused to look away and give him the satisfaction of knowing he was disconcerting her.

'Weren't you ever taught how to say please?'

Her hands clenched in her pockets. 'Where is my car?' she repeated, trying to keep the tremor out of her voice.

'Tut, tut, Cassie. You used to have such wonderful powers of persuasion.'

'Damn you,' she burst out. 'You forced me to stay here last night, but I'm damned if I'll spend another night under your roof!' Suddenly she felt dangerously close to breaking point. She caught her lip between her teeth to stop it trembling.

'What's the matter? Worried about what McAllister will think?'

She turned away, swallowing hard. *'Where is my car?'*

He watched her for a moment from under narrowed lids, then, 'Over there. Willis is taking a look at it.'

He nodded towards a row of garage doors, one of which stood open to reveal the blue Metro backed up on to a makeshift ramp, and without looking at Ross again she walked across to it, feeling his eyes boring into her back every inch of the way.

Willis was straightening his long length from beneath the car, his face impassive, and she made an effort to relax her own taut features into something resembling a smile as she gave him a stilted 'good morning' and offered him her thanks for getting the car out of the ditch.

He picked a rag off the bench and began to wipe his hands on it. 'That's all right, miss, but I'm afraid if you're hoping to drive anywhere today you're going to be sadly disappointed.'

She stared at him, suddenly still. 'What do you mean?'

'There's been some damage——'

'I know about the paintwork, Willis, but that won't stop me driving it, surely?'

'I'm afraid it's more than that, miss. The tank's ruptured.'

Cassie looked blank. 'The tank?'

'The petrol tank, miss. There's a big hole in it. Petrol's all gone.'

'But—can you fix it?'

''fraid not, miss. It's a garage job.'

A garage job! Cassie tried not to let Willis see the earth-shattering effect his words had had on her. Oh, God, why hadn't she stayed at home?

'Where's the nearest garage, Willis? How long will it take them to come out here?'

Willis gave her a pitying look. 'There's no garages open on a Sunday, miss, not up here. And as for coming out——' He shook his head, pursing his lips thoughtfully. 'I could perhaps give you a tow with the Land Rover in the morning, miss.'

'And how long will it take the garage to fix the tank?'

'The car'll have to have a new tank, miss. Depends if the garage has one in stock. They might have to send away to the main dealers——'

'And where is the nearest main dealer?' she interrupted fraughtly. It was an effort to keep the desperation out of her voice now.

Willis pursed his lips again. ''Appen there's one in Lancaster, miss.'

'*Lancaster?*' Cassie gave a groan of despair and sagged back against the car, cursing herself anew for rushing up here this weekend and getting herself into such an awful situation. She could have phoned first—or written a letter, anything that would have saved her from this mess! But her stupid desire to see Ross again had sent her rushing off on this crazy mission, and look where it had got her! She pushed her fingers through her hair and stared helplessly at the car, once again feeling ridiculously close to tears.

'Looks like you'll be staying another night, after all.'

Ross's voice from just behind her made her swing round furiously, eyes blazing, as temper overcame everything else.

'You knew about this, didn't you?' she accused, and his mocking smile gave her the answer. 'Why didn't you tell me?'

'You didn't ask.'

'Well, I'm not staying here,' she declared recklessly. 'I'll find a hotel—a guest-house—anything!'

His smiled disappeared. 'Don't be ridiculous! You'll stay here for as long as it takes. It'll do McAllister good to sweat a little.' He turned abruptly to make his way back across the cobbles, but she went after him, catching his arm and facing him furiously.

'That's all you can think about, isn't it? This stupid vendetta against me and the Bretts! What if I told you that Neil hasn't a clue where I am? That I haven't even seen him for the last three weeks?'

'I'd say that you were lying,' he replied tautly, and flung her hand off his arm. 'You must take me for a complete fool, Cassie! McAllister is your stepfather's right-hand man, he has dinner at your house damn near every night, he's like one of the family—and the poor sod's crazy about you! Even when you were with me he was always sticking his nose in. No, he knows where you are all right, and the longer you're here the madder he'll be, and unless you behave I might just decide to extend your visit!'

The threat behind his words was unmistakable, and Cassie paled. 'You wouldn't——'

'Just try me!' he muttered tightly. 'After all, this place is pretty isolated...'

'You're despicable!' she blazed, and he smiled grimly.

'On the contrary, we used to have some good times together—or have you conveniently forgotten all those afternoons we spent at my flat?'

She felt as though he'd dealt her a physical blow as pain lanced through her heart. How could he refer to those times so coldly—taunt her so cruelly?

'Besides——' he continued softly. 'If you made up your mind to be a little more—amenable, I could even make it worth your while——'

She took a step back, gasping, and her hand flew up to slap his face, but her aim was wide, and even before her palm could make contact he had caught her wrist and jerked her forcibly against him.

'Just remember, Cassie,' he grated, 'any more of your lies and deceit and you'll find out just how despicable I can really be!'

Cassie stared miserably at her suitcase standing open on the ottoman at the foot of the bed, still neatly packed from this morning, and wished desperately for an excuse to stay in her room—anything to avoid the evening ahead. She was filled with cold dread at the thought of getting dressed, going down for dinner, and having to face Ross again.

She was a prisoner, she realised desperately, tied to the whims of a man who was out of control, unpredictable, and hell-bent on her destruction, and that he could destroy her she had no doubt. She was already on the edge. One more word from Ross could shatter her into a thousand million pieces, and she was terrified. She had even contemplated locking herself in her room, but there was no lock on the door—there didn't seem to be locks on any of the doors, and she had no doubt that if she didn't appear he would lose no time in coming to find her. The ball was firmly in his court, and he had made it disastrously clear this morning that if she didn't play the game his way the consequences would be dire.

And she had no trouble in believing the threat behind his words. After last night, she could believe anything. Discovering that the man she had loved had used her so callously was a soul-destroying revelation. She had been out on the hill all afternoon, wandering aimlessly, struggling to find a thread of sanity in all this, but the gathering dusk had driven her back to the house, still uncomprehendingly numb.

And she still had to face him tonight.

Well, at least she didn't have to worry about what to wear. She'd only brought one dress with her, never thinking her evenings would be such formal occasions. But no doubt Elise would be wearing something exotic, and Cassie had enough to do with the thought of facing Ross again, without having to put up with derisive glances from Elise Maxwell, as she had done this morning.

It was Elise who had broken up the scene in the yard. She had appeared from the direction of the kitchen, looking absolutely stunning in a silk shirt and couture trousers, a cashmere sweater draped across her shoulders, and stopped dead at the sight of Cassie struggling with Ross in the middle of the yard.

What she had thought of their arguing in such close proximity Cassie could only imagine, but the look Elise had given her had spoken volumes. However, the estimable Elise was Ross's problem, and on seeing her approach he had been forced to release Cassie—with a muffled oath—and she had hastily made her escape, staying well out of the way until she saw them drive away in Elise's expensive two-seater Mercedes sports.

Dora had told her that Ross and Mrs Maxwell were staying out for lunch, and Cassie had thankfully eaten her own lunch in the kitchen under Dora's watchful eye. But there would be no such escape at dinner, and abruptly Cassie got up to move across to her suitcase and pull out the knitted dress.

It was a soft mohair mix in subtle shades of green, with a cowl neck and long sleeves; a warm dress, one she always felt comfortable in, and she had brought it thinking it would be ideal for the cold autumn evenings—little realising just how cold those evenings were going to be.

At least she had the consolation of knowing Ross would be reasonably civil to her in Elise's presence, but that would be cold comfort when those grey eyes could slice through her like a knife, and she would be constantly reminded of what he had insinuated this morning.

And after dinner—what then? Would she be allowed to leave them alone? Surely she didn't have to sit with them *all* evening? She was tense enough already, her nerves stretched to an almost unbearable degree, without having to spend all evening trying to disguise the surging emotions that were threatening to tear her to pieces.

Having to stay here one night had been bad enough. Knowing she had to stay two, or even three or four nights, was unbearable. She had never wanted to escape from anywhere so much in her life—and never had escape seemed so impossible, her walk on the hill this afternoon had told her that. The place was completely iso-

lated, and she was trapped here with a man who hated
her to the point of insanity.

And insanity it had to be, she had decided. She didn't
know anything about the missing designs, and she
wouldn't until she returned to London, but of one thing
she was sure—her stepfather wouldn't have had anything to do with it. James was too honest, too open. He
would never even consider anything so despicable. And
as for Grandfather Brett—well, she knew there were
shady areas in his life. He had said himself, more than
once, that there were things he regretted in his past; but
he had always been able to inspire trust in the people
who worked with him and she couldn't believe that he
would ever deliberately betray that trust—and certainly
not in such a cruel and callous fashion.

As for Ross's accusations against *her*...she pushed
her fingers through her hair in a weary movement.

She had gone over and over the events of two years
ago in her mind, trying to reason out how Ross could
possibly have come to the fantastic conclusion that she
had walked out on him, and completely failed. There
was nothing—*nothing* that had seemed at all unusual.
If it hadn't been for the look in his eyes, the bitterness
in his voice, she could almost believe that it was some
trumped-up charge he had invented against her to cover
his own despicable behaviour...

The irony of it was, she had wanted to die herself at
the time, but, apart from concussion, she hadn't even
been badly injured. As Bill Hodges had said, the driver's
side of the car had taken the full force of that oncoming
vehicle. What had actually happened was still a blank,
but she could remember being with Ross on that final
evening. The next thing she knew she was in hospital,

with her mother at her side, and the knowledge that Ross was dead. She'd been made to stay in hospital for a couple of days, and then arrangements had been made to move her to a private clinic. There had been no inkling that everything was not as it seemed. And yet here was a man, a living, breathing image of Ross, who refused to believe anything she said and twisted everything against her. He had to be insane—and the thought of spending the next three or four days under his roof was driving her out of her mind.

When she was ready she made her way slowly down to the sitting-room, hesitating at the door, her hand on the knob; but all was quiet and she went in. She thought at first that the room was empty, but Elise was there, draped across the armchair nearest the fire, her crimson-tipped fingers already curled around a half-filled glass. She turned as Cassie entered, but didn't speak, merely moving her head slightly in haughty acknowledgement of Cassie's presence, and without a word Cassie went across to the drinks cabinet and poured herself a large brandy, her fingers shaking as she added a dash of lemonade. She was raising the glass to her lips when Elise's soft drawl drifted across the room.

'Top mine up, would you, dear?'

Setting her own glass down again, untouched, Cassie turned. Elise was holding out her glass, smiling silkily.

'Bacardi and lemonade, dear. With ice.'

Cassie fixed the drink and handed it back, feeling Elise's eyes on her all the while, curious, speculative, but she didn't return the look. She didn't want to have anything to do with Elise, and she certainly had no intention of satisfying her curiosity. She settled herself in the armchair on the opposite side of the hearth and took a sip of her brandy, and there was a silence. Then Elise spoke again.

'Tell me, have you know Ross long?'

Cassie stared into her glass. 'Long enough.'

'I'm surprised we've never met before—Cassie, isn't it?' Cassie nodded, and Elise continued, 'I've known Ross for ages, since he first came to live with his uncle. In fact, we were almost engaged to be married at one time.'

Cassie looked up then, and Elise's dark eyes glinted at her, catlike in the firelight.

'What happened?' Cassie asked, knowing she was expected to and unable to help herself.

Elise's slim shoulders were raised in a little shrug. 'Oh, you know how it is. Ross got a job on a London paper, and before I knew what was happening, David—David Maxwell, that is, my late husband—had appeared on the scene and whisked me off to California. But Ross and I never lost touch. As soon as he decided to come back here to live he called me and asked me to help him with the house. I'm an interior designer, you know.' She paused. 'What do you do?'

'I work in a boutique.'

Elise's expertly mascaraed lashes flicked over the mohair dress. 'Really?' she said, and Cassie read a wealth of meaning behind that one word. She lowered her eyes, taking another sip of her brandy to cover the sudden bubble of hysterical amusement that rose inside her. Perhaps it was just as well she wasn't wearing one of Natalie's designs. If Elise knew exactly what her work at the boutique entailed...

'Well, as I was saying, Ross wanted some ideas for the house,' Elise continued, settling herself more comfortably. 'It's a shame it's been let to go to rack and ruin like this——' She flicked her wrist at the room in general. 'Ross adored his uncle, of course, but the old man was quite batty—an eccentric recluse,' she added, at Cassie's questioning look. 'You never met him?'

Cassie shook her head

'Well, by the time *dear* old Uncle Nick left it all to Ross there was hardly anything left that was worth having, but now, with all the money he's made from his book, Ross has decided to restore it to its former glory.' She twirled her glass between her fingers, watching Cassie from beneath lowered lids. 'You know about the book, of course?'

Cassie tried not to look as blank as she felt. Ross had written a book? She vaguely remembered him saying once that he was working on some ideas, and when he finally gave up chasing half-way across the world after front page news, then he'd turn to writing. But Elise had picked up that first flash of surprise.

'Oh, yes! All those political stories he was always un-covering? Well, he put a few of them together and turned them into a thriller. It's an absolute blockbuster from all accounts. You must have heard of Nicholas Breck!'

'Nicholas Breck?' Cassie echoed faintly. 'You mean—*Ross* is Nicholas Breck?' Who hadn't heard of the author whose book had caused a furore in government circles and been at the top of the bestseller list almost from the day it came out, and there was already talk of it being made into a film.

Elise rattled on and Cassie stared at her in dazed sur-prise. It was as though Elise was talking about an ab-solute stranger. Her senses last night had been right—she hadn't really known Ross at all in those few brief months. He had swept into her life, swept her off her feet, and she had been in such a daze that she had never thought to question the deeper, more complex side of his personality. She took a gulp of her brandy and Elise sat back, looking smugly satisfied.

'Of course, I always knew he had it in him. He's already working on another book, you know. He says it'll be even better than the first.' She sipped delicately at her glass. 'Well, now he can afford to do as he pleases, but for some reason he seems intent on doing this place up.' She let her gaze drift round the room. 'Silly, isn't it? This place is so isolated, but he won't hear of moving nearer to London. He's talking about settling down at last.' She looked back at Cassie and smiled, and Cassie received her second shock. Elise was telling her that Ross was doing the house up for *her*?

'Of course, it will take time. David hasn't been dead a year, you know,' she said, as if to reinforce the message. 'But the kitchen is already finished, and now we're discussing what to do with the dining-room. But our ideas are so completely in agreement, it'll be no time at all before the whole house is restored, and then...'

Cassie could take no more. She stood up quickly— too quickly, and her glass slipped from her fingers and smashed on to the hearth. Trembling, she bent to gather the scattered fragments and mop up what was left of the alcohol with her handkerchief, before going back to the drinks cabinet to pour herself another brandy with shaking fingers.

And then suddenly Ross himself was there, framed in the open doorway and leaning heavily on the sticks, surveying them both from beneath narrowed lids.

'I see you two are having a cosy little fireside chat,' he drawled, and Cassie looked away, feeling the heat come into her cheeks at his tone. But Elise seemed completely unmoved by this cryptic remark.

'Ross, darling, I was just telling your—er—friend about our plans for the house.'

'And what did she say—or can I guess?' Ross's voice was heavy with sarcasm as he manoeuvred himself further into the room.

But Elise continued blithely, 'Well, she didn't say anything really, but when I told her about the book she was absolutely stunned.'

'I'll bet she was!' Ross's narrowed look had snapped to Cassie and she felt herself flushing even further.

'It's true!' she burst out, glaring back at him. 'I didn't know anything about it—for heaven's sake, why won't you believe *anything* I say——?'

She stopped as abruptly as she'd begun, suddenly realising how she must sound, how it must look to Elise. The other woman was already staring at her in amazement. And anyway, what was the point in arguing with Ross? Hadn't she already decided he was out of his mind?

His eyes had moved down to the glass in her hand. 'I didn't know you were addicted to brandy, Cassie,' he bit out.

So he thought she was drunk, did he? Recklessly Cassie raised the glass to her lips and took another gulp of the fiery liquid, completely forgetting that this time it was neat, and choking as it caught her throat.

It was a moment before she could regain her breath, and there was an embarrassed silence. Ross was staring at her in icy disapproval, and Elise began in sly amusement, 'Really, Ross, you know the strangest people! I had no idea she knew nothing about the...'

Ross turned back to Elise and her voice withered and died under his look. Her beautiful mouth took on a petulant twist, but Ross's voice, when it came, was chillingly smooth.

'Dora's ready to serve. Shall we go through to the dining-room?'

Dinner was eaten in comparative silence, but afterwards, back in the sitting-room drinking coffee, Elise began to talk again, this time discussing various colour schemes for the dining-room with Ross. She sat next to him on the sofa, her hand on his knee, her face close to his, effectively excluding Cassie from the conversation, and Cassie sat at the other end of the room, sipping her coffee in brooding silence.

But when Elise suggested getting out the sample-books, Ross shook his head, frowning, and Cassie's eyes were drawn to his face, once again noticing the deeply etched lines, the tightness round his eyes and mouth. Elise's eyes, too, were still fixed on Ross's face, but now she was suggesting a game of backgammon—apparently this was how they had spent the last couple of evenings. But once again Ross shook his head, and now the grey eyes were glinting in Cassie's direction.

'Cassie always used to enjoy a game of backgammon, didn't you, Cassie?' And before Cassie could object she found herself seated opposite a furious Elise, while Ross settled himself in the armchair by the fire, his long legs stretched out to the blaze, his gaze fixed broodingly on the flames.

Cassie played a hopeless game. She was in no mood for backgammon, she couldn't concentrate; she was too aware of the man by the fire, of the long, lean length of him, the dark head resting against the soft fabric of the armchair, the firelight playing over the harsh lines of his face and glinting in the depths of the grey eyes, partly veiled by the heavy lids. Even as she watched, a spasm crossed the dark features, and she felt a jolt go through her. Was he in pain—perhaps from those shattered legs? He shifted restlessly in the chair, easing his long length slightly, bending his knee and wincing at the movement. She looked away, suddenly shocked by the urge to touch him, to let her fingers soothe those lines of strain from his face.

Shaken, she stared unseeingly down at the backgammon board. What on earth was the matter with her, for heaven's sake? A couple of hours ago she had been terrified, desperate to get away, and now, because she thought he was in pain, all she wanted to do was comfort him!

She looked across at Elise. The other woman was oblivious of Ross, concentrating on the game, determined to win, and Cassie's eyes flicked back to Ross.

He was prone to migraines, she knew. She remembered once how, after a particularly gruelling assignment, she had gone to meet him at the flat. She had been shocked at the sight of him, and they had sat on the rug in the firelight, his head in her lap, while her fingers soothed the tension from his aching temples. He had lain there, eyes closed, and she had thought at first he was asleep, but then, eyes darkening, he had smiled up at her and pulled her down on to the rug...

Elise's voice brought her back to the present with a jerk and she stared at the other girl blankly.

'It's your throw,' Elise repeated, her irritation obvious, and Cassie hastily reached for the dice, her cheeks hot, as she realised exactly where her thoughts had been leading her.

She couldn't understand it. The knowledge of Ross's vulnerability should have elated her, made her feel revengefully satisfied, but instead there was a curious ache inside her that refused to be shifted, and she found herself watching him from under her lashes, noting the lines of strain around his mouth, searching for any further signs of discomfort.

She turned back to find Elise watching her, the dark eyes maliciously intent, and she pulled herself together, forcing her mind back to the game in hand, telling herself she was a fool.

Not unexpectedly—at least, not to Cassie—Ross bid them an abrupt goodnight just after ten o'clock, and Elise, with a sly look at Cassie, decided she, too, would retire. Cassie was left to put the game away and she did so mechanically, automatically moving round the board to collect up the dice and men before carrying them across to the hearthrug and kneeling in the dying warmth of the fire while she fitted the pieces into their separate compartments in the box. She was preoccupied, disturbed by the realisation that Ross's vulnerability should still affect her, and as she worked she tried to analyse her own confused emotions. But she was tired and her brain refused to co-operate. It kept wandering off at a tangent, as it had done earlier, conjuring up pictures of a man who, it seemed now, had never existed.

It was as though she was torn in two. One half of her was still living in the past, remembering the lover she had once known, while the other half was painfully in the present, berating her for being a fool, for feeling anything for this callous stranger, this man who was beyond all reason, and so intent was she on her own thoughts that it was a moment before she realised the door had opened again and Ross had reappeared.

It was obvious he didn't know she was there, and she realised, too, that he wasn't using his sticks. The effort it cost him to cross the room held her riveted.

He reached the drinks cabinet and stopped, leaning heavily against it, and then a log fell in the fire and he turned and saw her. There was silence for a moment as they stared at each other, and then he said in a low, hard voice, 'What do you think you're doing?'

'I was putting the game away.' She straightened as she spoke, the box in her hands.

'I thought you'd gone to bed!' He produced a pill box from his pocket and shook a couple of capsules out on to his palm. She watched him, mesmerised; but as though he could feel that her eyes were still on him he paused and looked up, raising a sardonic eyebrow in her direction, and abruptly she turned and went across to the cupboard she'd seen Elise take the backgammon board from earlier. By the time she'd put the game away and straightened again, he was gulping down the capsules with a tumbler of something he'd taken from the cabinet.

She stared at him, horrified. 'Don't you know you shouldn't mix drugs and alcohol?' she exclaimed.

He turned to her again, the glass still raised. 'Concerned for my welfare, Cassie?' he remarked sarcastically, and she stiffened.

'It's common sense, that's all. You'll end up killing yourself——'

'And finishing what you started?' he bit back. 'That would be very convenient, wouldn't it? You ought to be on the stage, Cassie, you'd make a fortune——'

'And you ought to be in a lunatic asylum!' she flung back at him, bitter anger in her own voice now. 'This vendetta you're so intent on—it's—it's madness! You must be crazy even to consider it——'

'Changed your tactics now, have you?' he derided harshly. 'Or have you simply decided that attack is the best form of defence?'

She was silenced, staring at him. That steel band was across her chest again, crushing her heart, squeezing the very life blood out of it.

'I've nothing to defend,' she declared tautly. 'Nothing that I'm ashamed of, anyway.'

His face darkened furiously and he took a couple of steps towards her, coming up against the back of the sofa and clenching his fist against the soft cushions. 'By God, Cassie, I'll make you pay for that. That you can stand there and say that to my face——'

'I say it because it's the *truth*!' she retorted fiercely. 'I loved you, Ross——'

'So it was all a big mistake, was it? You never *meant* to leave me? You'll be trying to tell me next that you would have married me anyway!'

She swung away, raking her fingers through her hair in a futile movement of despair. 'Yes—*yes*, I would have married you!' she responded bitterly. 'I would have married you even if you'd been a heap of *nothing*—and if you'd loved me even just a little you would have known that I could never—*never*——'

'Never what? Never come to me and tell me how you felt? Never tell me to my face that you didn't want me

any more?' he demanded harshly. 'I set you apart,
Cassie. I thought you were completely different from
the rest of that devil's brood you have for a family—
that's some measure of just how besotted I really was.
But it was all a con, wasn't it? One big con from start
to finish. Tell me, was I getting too hot? Was I getting
too close to the *real* truth? Is that why they decided to
bring you in, as some kind of diversion while they got
rid of the evidence?'

'There was no evidence!' she got out. 'At least—not
at Brett's, and if anyone was conned it was me—for believing that you wanted me for what I was, not *who* I
was! I was better off believing you were *dead*——'

'Even if I had been, I would have come back from
hell to haunt you!' he interrupted grimly. 'I'll not rest
until this thing is settled, Cassie, and if you think I'm
going to conveniently poison myself with drink and
drugs, then you can think again! I never take anything
stronger than soda water with my tablets, and with what
I need to kill the pain I'd be a fool to do otherwise. See
for yourself!'

He thrust the tumbler towards her and she stared at
it, before raising her eyes to the bitter pain in his face.
Then, with a cry of frustrated anguish, she turned and
slammed out of the room and up to bed.

CHAPTER FOUR

THE next morning dawned bright once more, but by the time Cassie had eaten breakfast the clouds were gathering, and by ten o'clock it was raining steadily. She sat in the Land Rover next to Willis as they wound their way down to the garage, staring out at the damp landscape and thinking that Saturday night, when she had driven up this road in the rain, seemed like an eternity ago.

London seemed suddenly dearly familiar, and she resolved to find a phone and call Elaine, away from the listening walls at The Breck. Ross seemed adept at appearing, apparently out of nowhere, and she had no wish for him to overhear her conversation with her mother, which she knew would be explosive. Elaine didn't even know she was away from London. Cassie had had the vague idea of coming up here and somehow returning to London before her mother even discovered her absence; but now, with her car off the road, that was out of the question, and Elaine would be furious, she knew. Neil was due back from the States some time in the next two days and she would be expected to be on hand to welcome him.

At the thought of Neil she sighed heavily and stared miserably through the streaming windscreen. This weekend had taught her one thing at least—she knew now that she could never marry Neil. He was a good friend, yes, but anything else would be a mistake. Seeing

Ross again had made her realise how much her relationship with Neil lacked. There was no spark—not on her side, at least—and Neil was so undemonstrative, so cool. He was more like a brother than anything else, and perhaps that was the problem. He still treated her as some kind of overgrown child. She would probably have been bored to death within a couple of years—well on the way to following in Julia's footsteps, and look how *her* marriage was turning out. But then, if it hadn't been for Ross...

The garage, when they reached it, seemed little more than a couple of petrol pumps, with a piece of waste ground at the back containing various parts of tractors and a couple of council lorries; but Willis seemed on good terms with the mechanic, whom he introduced as George. Willis explained that Cassie wanted to return to London as soon as possible, and George nodded and winked at Cassie, and said he didn't think it was much of a job. There were some jocular remarks about lady drivers, to which Willis retained his usual stony-faced imperturbability, and then Cassie left him in the ramshackle office discussing the state of the weather while she ran across the road to a public phone box.

As she had guessed, Elaine was furious and demanded to know her whereabouts, but Cassie was prepared for this and managed to remain suitably vague. She had no intention of telling her mother about Ross— at least, not yet. There would be time enough to reopen old hostilities in that direction when she returned to London. At the moment she had enough with her own tangled emotions without having to cope with what she dreaded would be a furious 'I told you so!' from Elaine. And anyway, she only had two ten-pence pieces with her and the call was mercifully short. Elaine was cut off in mid-flow by the tone.

On the drive back to the house she began to feel her spirits lifting a little, and she told herself it was because she was finally in sight of going home again. Her inability to escape from The Breck had caught her on the raw, but now, at least, the car was in the garage, and with any luck, by tomorrow evening she would be on her way home. Even Willis's granite features seemed more inclined to friendliness, but this fragile mood was shattered as they pulled into the yard to see Elise leaning nonchalantly against her gleaming red car, and Ross coming slowly out of the house to join her.

Willis brought the Land Rover to a halt and jumped out to help the other man, while Cassie climbed out more slowly, moving to stand silently by the bonnet, her hands in her pockets.

Ross and Willis were murmuring together in an undertone, and then Ross nodded, apparently satisfied. Willis helped him into the Mercedes' passenger seat while Elise sauntered round to the driver's door.

'We'll probably eat out,' Ross informed Dora, who had followed him out. 'But whatever happens, we won't be late back.'

'Oh, no,' Elise murmured, with a little shudder. 'I hate driving in the dark!'

She slid gracefully down into the driver's seat, and then the full force of Ross's gaze was turned on Cassie.

'Dora and Willis will look after you,' he said, and Cassie's fingers balled into fists in her pockets at his tone.

'Oh, and by the way, your boots are ready,' he added, coolly mocking. 'Dora's cleaned them and put them in the hall. But I wouldn't go for any walks today if I were you. It's far too wet.'

Cassie glared at him, about to tell him she'd do as she damn well pleased, but Elise was already accelerating out of the yard and she could only glare impotently after them.

The rain eased after lunch, and in spite of what Ross had said, or perhaps because of it, she set out for a walk. But today the hills were obscured by low cloud, and when it began to drizzle again she was forced to turn back. Dora set her a tray of tea in the study, but sitting there, in that room in Ross's house, her own thoughts were too intrusive, and after a while she got up to pace restlessly round the room, before finally picking a couple of books at random off the shelves and flinging herself down in the armchair again in an attempt to read.

The emotions of the weekend were finally beginning to take their toll, she realised desolately. She was on tenterhooks all the time, watching, listening, waiting for Ross to reappear. If only her car could be ready *today*...

One of the books was an old copy of Wordsworth's selected poems, and she flicked it open, only to see a name inscribed across the top corner of the flyleaf. It took her a moment to decipher the faded ink, and then she stared at it in stunned disbelief. Nicholas Daleford, it read. Was this Ross's uncle—the engineer?

She could hear her mother's voice, as though she was sitting next to her, announcing bitterly, 'If I hadn't worked myself up to become personal assistant to Mr Daleford, we would never have had any money for anything...'

Cassie snapped the book shut. She felt suddenly sick. It was a coincidence—it had to be. Ross's uncle and the

man her mother had worked for in Manchester were two
completely different people—weren't they?

Abruptly she got up to put the book back on the shelf,
before turning back to survey the rest of the room
through narrowed eyes, as though seeing it for the first
time, while her mind went back through the years to
when her family had lived in Manchester.

She had only been a child then, of course, and she
couldn't remember a time when her mother *hadn't* gone
out to work, but even so, most of the details of whom
her mother worked for, even the firm itself, had passed
over her head—or, if she had known them, they were
long forgotten. Besides, at the time her young mind had
been focused on what to her were far more important
things. It was strange how children were always the first
to know and the last to be told when their parents were
on the point of breaking up.

But surely, if there were any clues, they would be found
here, in this house, Nicholas Daleford's old home?

She moved across to the desk. A couple of the drawers
were locked, but a quick look through the others told
her there was nothing of interest here. They were mostly
full of files and notebooks belonging to Ross, and apart
from forcing the two locked drawers there was nowhere
else she could look.

Anyway, no doubt Ross had already disposed of most
of his uncle's stuff, she realised belatedly, and if there
was anything of any importance relating to Nicholas
Daleford's firm, and the people who had worked for
him, Ross would have it safely locked away somewhere,
not lying around here waiting for her to find it. Deflated
again, she straightened.

The afternoon was drawing in, and she flicked on the desk-lamp, while her eyes wandered over the papers strew over its leather-topped surface. She picked up a word here and there, and then stiffened, realising suddenly what it was she was looking at. She picked up a couple of sheets, reading quickly, and then moved to read what was in the typewriter, sinking down into the deep-buttoned swivel chair that was positioned behind the desk.

This was Ross's manuscript, his second novel, the one Elise had said would be even better than the first. But most of the typing had been crossed out or altered, and when she looked at some of the other typewritten sheets, whole sections had been scored out, while others had remarks and copious notes scribbled over them in Ross's hand. The waste-paper basket, too, was overflowing with crumpled sheets of paper, some with only a couple of lines typed on them, blank, meaningless prose that lacked the force, the sparkle that she had always associated with Ross's work.

He was obviously going through a bad patch with his writing—and if he knew she had seen this he would be furious! But even as she hastily stood up again to move away from the desk, the door was flung open and Ross himself stood there, his eyes blazing.

'What the hell do you think you're doing?'

His anger hit her like a blast from a furnace, and unconsciously she backed away from the desk. 'I'm sorry, I didn't realise——'

'Like hell you didn't! Who let you in here?'

'There was no fire in the sitting-room, and Dora said——'

'Well, Dora should have had more sense!' He was manoeuvring himself over to the desk, gathering up the half-typed sheets, the scribbled notes. 'It's bad enough having you snooping round the rest of the house, appearing everywhere like some damned ghost, without having you prying in here at things that don't concern you.'

'I was not prying!' she retorted, guiltily aware that that was exactly what she had been doing, but she couldn't let Ross know of her suspicions concerning her own mother. 'If you don't want people to see your precious manuscript, then you shouldn't leave it lying about!' she muttered defensively.

He placed his knuckles on the desk and leaned across, glaring at her. 'This is *my* study,' he underlined grimly, 'and until now it has been respected as such. Dora and Willis know enough to keep away when I'm working, and until *you* came I never had to worry about keeping everything under lock and key!'

He hadn't mentioned Elise, Cassie thought, as a stab of bitter fire ran through her, but she pushed that aspect of it aside. She couldn't think about that now. 'Well, I wasn't prying!' she repeated—not into his manuscript, anyway. 'And besides, you're forgetting, until last night I didn't even know you'd turned to writing books—that your work was such a success——'

'Still play-acting, Cassie?' His lip had curled back into a contemptuous sneer. 'I'm not quite as gullible as Elise. No doubt you didn't know either how much money I was making!'

'I never gave it a thought!' she flung at him, hopelessly aware that he wouldn't believe her even if she told him the sky was blue. 'I'm simply surprised you've made such a success of your life when you're so twisted up inside!'

His eyebrows rose, derisively mocking. 'You prefer to think of me pining away up here for love of you, is that it?' he questioned sarcastically, and she flung away from him towards the hearth, exasperation, anger, pain warring inside her and making it impossible for her to continue. And what was the point? He always had the last word, anyway! Was there no way she could get through to him?

His eyes had narrowed speculatively. 'Come to think of it, I wouldn't put it past Elaine to have sent you up here this weekend, hoping for a reconciliation. She always did have an eye to the main chance where her daughters were concerned—you only have to look at the poor sucker who's married to Julia to see that! Roddy may have money—but that's about all he has got! Admittedly I'm not in the same league as Neil McAllister—if you married him it would tie the family firm up very nicely—keep it in the family, so to speak. But on the other hand, a bestselling author is quite a conversation piece—even though he is half crippled——'

'Stop it—*stop it*!' she gasped, and put her hands up to cover her ears; but, though she could shut out his words, she couldn't stop the now familiar clenching of her stomach muscles, the steel band closing painfully across her chest, and every bitter word he threw at her seemed to make the pain more unbearable. He was tearing her to pieces, destroying her as he had said he would.

'*Why* are you doing this?' she choked. 'Why—*why*?'

'I think that should be *my* line,' he retorted caustically. 'You're the one who's insisting on continuing with this charade.'

'But it's *not* a charade! *Why* won't you believe me?' She turned back to face him again, spreading her hands in earnest supplication, her eyes wide and brimming with unshed tears as she searched his face for a sign, a glimmer of the tenderness she had once known; but his features were as hard and unyielding as stone.

And yet she needed to talk to him, she realised starkly. She needed to reason with him, to break through that mask and try and discover some inkling of the Ross she had known.

She took a step towards him, swallowing painfully. 'Ross—— ' she began. 'Ross, you're a reporter, you deal in facts. You're trained to uncover the truth. I can't believe you're acting like this! Treating me so—so——'

'And how do you expect me to treat you?' he bit out, sinking down into the swivel chair. 'You left me. I know *that* for a fact. You threw me away like a broken toy. And as for the other—I'll not throw you out to freeze to death on the hills, have no fear of that. You can expect the bare essentials of hospitality, but certainly no more!'

'The bare essentials of hospitality——?' she choked. 'You're keeping me a *prisoner*!'

His eyebrows rose, chillingly aloof. 'A prisoner? You're deluding yourself. What about your trip to the garage this morning? You could have left any time you'd wanted to.'

She stared at him. The garage! Of course—why hadn't she thought of it before? And she'd made a phone call— she could have phoned for a taxi, or a car—she stopped, shoulders suddenly slumping. There'd been no directories of any kind in the kiosk, and there'd been no cars that she could see at the garage.

'And what about Willis?' she retorted acidly. 'Are you going to tell me he would have just let me walk away?'

'He let you walk across the road to the phone box, didn't he?' Ross pointed out, and now it was her turn to raise her eyebrows.

'I think that answers my question!' she snapped. '*Now* who's deluding himself?'

'You're making excuses——'

'No, it's you who's making excuses,' she contradicted bitterly. 'You won't even listen to reason! You're insisting on keeping me here just so that you can make me a victim for your twisted psychological games.' She drew a shaking breath. 'Tell me, Ross, did you *ever* love me? Even just a little?'

He got to his feet again then, his face pale and taut, and brought his fist down on the surface of the desk. 'By God, Cassie, if anyone's a victim in all this, it should be me! Yes, I loved you. That's what made it so damned hard. I couldn't believe you'd do it—not to me, the man you swore you'd marry!'

She was on the brink of tears. 'Then how can you believe it now?' she choked. 'I loved you, too—you know that in your heart! At least give me a hearing—let me explain what happened——'

'There's nothing to explain.' He seemed almost weary now. 'I heard it all in hospital.'

'But you can't have done—I wasn't there!' she pointed out desperately. 'At least give me a chance to defend myself—even Bill Hodges never doubted I was telling the truth!'

At the mention of Bill Hodges he looked up, and she pressed her advantage, continuing hurriedly, 'You said Bill Hodges phoned you after I'd been to see him? He must have told you how I reacted when I discovered you were still alive?' Her voice softened appealingly. 'Ross— these last months——'

'These last months I've been learning to walk again,' he interrupted harshly. 'Do you know how many bones were broken in my legs? How many operations I've had? Perhaps I should show you my scars some time.' He smiled grimly as she visibly flinched. 'Believe me, it's not a pretty sight.'

She was white-faced now, shaking. 'It's no worse than the sight of you wallowing in self-pity,' she retorted, and he spun round, his eyes narrowing dangerously.

'*What* did you say?'

She glared back, anger, frustration and bitter pain searing along her veins. She had had enough of his gibes; that last remark had cut her to the quick—and he knew it. Well, she could be cruel too.

'You're really enjoying yourself, aren't you?' she flung at him. 'Playing the martyr, trying to make me feel riddled with guilt, while all the while you're living up here—conveniently cut off from anyone who can testify to the truth, having cosy little weekends with your girl-friend——'

'You almost make it sound as though you're jealous!' he derided, and there was an unfathomable glint in the grey eyes.

'*Jealous?*' she gasped, and then his words sank in, lit up in her mind like a neon sign.

Yes, she was jealous. Bitterly, painfully, achingly jealous! Elise was here, with Ross, and she had no right to be...

But she couldn't be jealous—she couldn't be! To feel jealousy you had to feel love, too, didn't you? And she didn't love Ross now, she couldn't—not after all he'd said and done. *She couldn't.*

Shaken, confused, she turned away, trying not to let him see the tangle of emotions she was sure must be written on her face.

Did she still love him? Was that what all this pain was about? Love and hate ran parallel along either side of a fine line, and she thought she had crossed that line. She was convinced she hated him. But last night, after dinner, when she had thought he was in pain...

Her fists were clenched on her temples, almost as though her head was hurting unbearably. 'We loved each other once——' she began, and her voice was a whisper, almost an entreaty. 'We had something infinitely precious. I can't believe that you could turn your back on that, any more than I could——'

He turned away, swung round on the sticks with a sound almost of disgust, and when she looked up he was almost at the door.

'Just remember what I said,' he grated, his voice strangely hoarse. 'Keep out of here when I'm working.' And he slammed out before she could say another word.

That night she lay tossing and turning in the darkness, her brain a confusion of thoughts and feelings she hardly knew she was capable of, let alone understood.

She needed to get away, she thought desperately, now more than ever. Being shut up here with Ross was driving *her* insane too. Perhaps once she was back in London she would begin to find some answers, to see things in perspective. She would try and phone the garage in the morning, she decided, and see if her car was nearly ready, and in her dreams she was already driving away from The Breck, the steering wheel steady in her hands, the road stretching smooth and golden before her. Dusk was falling, a soft, dewy dusk that melted into a velvet blackness, and she flicked the car headlights on, searching for the road. The car seemed suddenly to be going much too fast, but she couldn't slow down, and as she gripped the steering wheel, searching the darkness ahead, she caught sight of another car hurtling towards her, its tyres screeching on the vicious bends.

She knew who was driving it. She could see his face, white and twisted in the glare of the headlights, and she searched desperately for a turning, a lay-by, anywhere where she could get away from what she knew was about to happen. But the road was bordered by high stone walls, channelling her towards the oncoming vehicle—those dazzling lights—that huge, monstrous face. She blinked in the glare, trying to turn her head away, but firm hands were gripping her shoulders, shaking her unmercifully, forcing her to open her eyes...

'*Cassie!* For God's sake——'

She blinked up into Ross's face, her body rigid with fear, but his face was real enough; pale in the lamplight, his brows drawn together in a heavy frown as he bent over her, his fingers biting painfully into the bones of her shoulders.

'It's all right, Cassie. You were dreaming.'

She relaxed back against the pillows, relief surging through her, and put a hand up to her damp forehead, but she was trembling so badly that her movements were jerky, uncoordinated, and with a muttered exclamation he pushed her hand away and smoothed the hair out of her eyes, his fingers firm and cool on her hot skin.

'That was some nightmare,' he remarked drily, and she nodded, swallowing to ease her throat.

'Tell me about it,' he ordered softly, but she shook her head.

'No——'

'Tell me about it,' he persisted, and now there was steely determination in his voice.

Reluctantly she obeyed, her voice still husky from sleep, and as she recalled the last vivid details she shuddered again and flung her arm across her eyes in an unconscious gesture, trying to shut out the memory of those white, twisted features, but he pulled her arm away so that he could watch her face.

'Is it always the same?'

She nodded. 'Oh, it doesn't always begin that way, but I always know what the ending is going to be——' She stopped, suddenly still. 'How do you know I've had it before?' she questioned, and turned her head on the pillow to stare at him. 'Do you have nightmares, too?' she asked huskily, and suddenly she was wide awake, intensely aware of his tousled hair, his body leaning across hers, his dressing-gown that only partly covered the dark, curling hairs of his chest.

As though suddenly aware of her scrutiny, he straightened. 'Not any more,' he muttered tightly, and stood up abruptly to limp across the width of the room, his hands thrust into his dressing-gown pockets.

She watched him, frowning, noticing suddenly that he was only using one stick. There was a silence.

'Would you like some coffee?' he said at last, turning to face her. 'I made a pot. I was just bringing it up when I heard you yelling blue murder in here.' And at her look of surprise, 'I couldn't sleep either,' he added, with a faint, derisive twist of his mouth.

'Oh——' she began. 'I'm sorry——'

But he interrupted harshly, 'Do you want that coffee or not?'

Without further hesitation she flung the covers back and made to get out of bed, unaccountably relieved because she was not to be left alone, then she stopped, electrified, brought to a sudden halt by the look on his face as the long length of her legs was unconsciously displayed to his gaze. She hastily pulled her nightdress down to cover her knees, but he was already turning away, tossing her dressing-gown to her as though nothing unusual had happened. But she felt as though she'd received an electric shock.

His bedroom was large and warm and suitably masculine in its décor—had this room, too, been completed before Elise arrived? Cassie wondered briefly. Two tall lamps stood either side of the enormous bed, casting their intimate glow over the rumpled sheets, the paperbacks piled up on the bedside-table, the ashtray with a waft of smoke still drifting upwards from a half-smoked cigarette.

Ross had moved some more books and files off the dressing-table and was plugging the percolator into a socket by the window. 'I'll fetch another cup,' he said, straightening, but Cassie was already taking a step backwards towards the door.

'I'll fetch it,' she began, hurriedly. 'If you'll tell me where the cups are——'

His look rooted her to the spot. 'I'm perfectly capable of fetching a cup from the kitchen!' he bit out, and she coloured, shifting uncomfortably from one foot to the other.

'I—I'm sorry, I didn't mean——'

He ran his fingers through his hair in exasperation. 'For God's sake, stop saying you're sorry. I'm not incapable, and even if I was I wouldn't want your damn pity.'

She opened her mouth, then closed it again and stared at the carpet. She couldn't tell him that pity had nothing to do with it. If anything, it was the sight of that huge bed that had made her suddenly, unaccountably nervous. She shouldn't have come, she realised now. This was dangerous territory. She could feel her nerves jumping every time he so much as looked in her direction; just because she had this foolish fear of being left alone...

'Sit down, for God's sake,' he directed harshly, and then, in a less aggressive tone, 'Stop hovering by the door. I'm not going to eat you—not tonight, anyway,' he added with a grim twist of his lips. 'But by the time I've told you which cupboard the cups are in I could have fetched one myself.'

His tone brought her back to her senses. He was right, she was acting like an overwrought schoolgirl. What could possibly happen? And besides—hadn't he made it perfectly clear what he thought of her?

He was already moving towards the door, and she pushed herself away from it and wandered disconsolately round to sit on the edge of the bed, her hands under her knees.

He had obviously been reading; there was a book facedown on the pillow, and she picked it up, flicking idly over the pages, settling herself more comfortably, her back against the pillows, her toes pushing down under the rumpled covers, seeking warmth. But she found the book heavy-going, and after skimming through a couple of pages she put it down again, smothering a yawn and unconsciously snuggling down still further into the warmth left by Ross's body.

It was strangely comforting, lying curled up in that huge bed, listening to the rain beating against the windows and the occasional gust of wind in the chimneys. She yawned again and closed her eyes, turning her face into the pillow, savouring the familiar smell, the masculine scent she had always associated with Ross. Memories drifted into her mind of when she was small and couldn't sleep, and she would creep into her parents' bed, wedging herself into the space between them, burrowing down into the warm darkness...

'What the hell do you think you're doing?'

Ross's voice from the doorway made her jerk upright, stammering in her confusion.

'I—I was waiting for you——'

Even as she said the words she realised how they must sound, and her face burned as his eyes narrowed dangerously, his glance flicking speculatively down the length of her body.

She leapt off the bed, at once horrified by what she had done and angry at the interpretation he had so obviously put on her actions.

She faced him, quivering. 'It—it's not what you think——'

'Isn't it? I'd say it's exactly what I think,' he bit out. 'From the minute you arrived here on Saturday night you've been throwing yourself at my head, using every trick in the book to get into my bed.'

She stared at him, open mouthed, quivering now with indignation. 'Don't you think you're confusing me with someone else?' she retorted acidly, and his brows jerked together.

'You've already made your jealousy of Elise very plain,' he snapped. 'But may I remind you that Elise is a guest in my house—an *invited* guest—and you are not!'

He took a menacing step towards her and she stepped back, but he was limping towards the dressing-table, banging the extra mug down with barely concealed violence. 'My God, it makes me sick the way you've wormed your way in here. You must have thought you'd really made it with that old nightmare routine——'

She stared disbelievingly at his back. 'You think it was a *trick*?'

'The oldest one in the book!'

She was speechless with rage, hurt, humiliation—and something else she couldn't quite fathom. That he could accuse her of behaving like some kind of wanton was bad enough—but that he could dismiss her nightmares as some kind of trickery... he was out of his mind! He was so obsessed by this stupid desire for revenge that he was twisting everything she said and did against her, even to the extent of believing she was still in love with him...

'You bastard!' she burst out. She was white-faced, shaking. 'You accuse *me* of playing tricks when I could accuse *you* of exactly the same! I almost believed you felt sorry for me back there—that the stone around what you have for a heart was actually beginning to crack a little—but all you wanted to do was get me into your bedroom——'

'If I'd wanted to seduce you I had the perfect opportunity just now!' He had turned back to face her, lip curling unpleasantly. 'That's a pretty lame excuse, Cassie, and you know it!'

'It's no lamer than your outrageous accusations!' She was shouting now, her voice wobbling ominously. She suddenly felt desperately close to tears.

His eyes narrowed. 'The next thing you'll be crying on my shoulder,' he jeered.

Her hands clenched in her pockets as she gulped back the sobs rising in her throat, struggling for control. Desolation was sweeping over her.

'Here——' he directed, thrusting one of the coffee-mugs towards her. 'Drink this. After all, it's what you came for—isn't it?'

Desolation was suddenly overcome by anger, a fierce, burning anger that made her want to strike out at him, hurt him, anything to wipe that despicable smile off his face, and she lashed out, striking the mug out of his hand in a fierce gesture of denial.

'*You know what you can do with your damn coffee——*'

The mug was knocked from his hand, sending its scalding contents down the front of his dressing-gown, and with an exclamation he stepped back, stumbling, crashing against the dressing-table and sending the percolator, books and the other mug crashing to the floor.

Cassie stood stock still, her hand flying to her mouth in horror.

'Oh, my God!' she breathed, and then, 'Ross—*Ross!* Are you all right?'

In a second she was kneeling by his side, sliding her arms under his shoulders, trying to lift him off the wet carpet. Of course it was a physical impossibility—even in the state he was in now he was far too heavy for her to be able to bear his weight, but he was already struggling to get up, swearing under his breath.

'Ross——' she gulped. 'Ross, I didn't mean——'

'Get away from me!' he exploded furiously. 'I know damn well what you meant—and I don't need your help——'

She managed to get him off the floor and he staggered across to the bed, sinking down on to it with a groan.

'Ross——' she choked. 'Are you hurt? *Ross——*'

He had collapsed backwards on the bed and she raced across to him, pulling frantically at the wet dressing-gown. His skin was already reddening in places, great patches of colour that seemed to burn before her very eyes. She had done First Aid at school and she desperately tried to think what to do, but her mind was blank with shock. As her gaze flicked helplessly round the room she noticed a door, opposite the one she had entered by, and hurriedly she moved towards it, praying it would be a bathroom. It was, and she grabbed the nearest towel and plunged it into the washbasin, turning the taps on full blast to soak it, before racing back to Ross and laying it gently across the already damp skin of his chest.

He was still lying across the bed, his face appearing almost grey in the lamplight. He was breathing heavily, but when he felt the towel across his chest he opened his eyes, struggling to sit up and pushing the towel away.

'My God, don't you think I'm wet enough?'

'But the coffee——'

'It hardly touched me! My dressing-gown took the brunt of it.' He was shrugging himself out of his dressing-gown as he spoke, revealing blue pyjama trousers, also damp and stained with coffee in places. Then suddenly he stopped what he was doing and seemed to listen.

'Have you left some water running?' he questioned sharply, and Cassie's head jerked round to the bathroom door.

'The taps!'

She flew back to the bathroom door and stared in horror at the overflowing washbasin. Already a good area of bathroom carpet was glistening with water, and she hurriedly turned the taps off before collapsing weakly against the tiled wall.

It was the shock, she told herself half hysterically, the shock of knowing that she had deliberately wanted to hurt Ross, but he had pushed her almost to the point of no return. His coldness, his cruel taunts, were more than she could bear...

She pushed herself away from the wall to peep round the bathroom door. He was still sitting on the bed, his brows drawn together in a black frown as he moved his hand cautiously over his damp chest. If he was seriously burned she would never forgive herself...

She reached for another towel and went back to stand in front of him.

'Here, use this,' she instructed, and held the towel out to him. He gave her a caustic look, but took it without a word and began to dry himself, wincing suddenly as he caught a tender area of skin.

She watched him. She needed to know if he was badly burned or not, and there was only one way to do that...

'Are you going to let me look at it?' she suggested coolly. 'Or do I have to go and wake Dora and Willis?' She felt sure he wouldn't want to do that. It would involve too many questions, too much speculation, especially combined with the debris round the dressing-table and the sodden bathroom carpet. And there was always the possibility that Elise would get to hear of it...

He glared at her for a moment, grey eyes clashing with green, and then flung the towel down with a muttered exclamation.

'There's hardly anything to look at——' he began, but she was already kneeling in front of him, running her fingers gently over the skin of his chest.

'Turn to the light,' she murmured, and then, 'Does this hurt?'

Her fingers had moved to a small patch of reddened skin just above his navel. It was hot and dry to the touch, and as her fingers moved gently round it she felt him shudder.

'It needs some cream——' she began, but the sentence was never finished. His hands had come up to cover hers, imprisoning her fingers against his skin, and the words died in her throat.

She tried to pull away, but the pressure of his hands tightened, preventing her from rising, and suddenly she was trembling. She stared at his fingers covering hers, hardly daring to breathe, overwhelmingly conscious of him, of his maleness.

'Cassie...' he breathed.

Slowly she dragged her gaze up to his. His eyes were dark, fixed on her face, her mouth.

Oh, no! she screamed silently. No, no!

His hands were moving to the swelling fullness of her breasts and she was unable to push them away. A shudder of excitement ran through her, but, even as his mouth began to descend to hers and her eyes closed in anticipation, she heard him groan, 'Oh, God!' and opened her eyes again.

Elise was stood in the doorway, dark hair tumbled round her beautiful face, and wearing a négligée that left nothing to the imagination.

'Ross—darling, I heard an awful noise. Is anything wrong?'

She stopped dead at the sight of Cassie, a look of almost incredulous amazement sweeping over her face, to be quickly replaced by something far more potent.

'My God!' she exploded, her tone completely different now from the husky words of a moment ago.

Cassie had leapt to her feet, backing against what was left of the dressing-table, but Ross seemed completely unmoved. His face resumed its normal mask and he stood up, turning slowly to face Elise.

'There's been an accident,' he said calmly. 'I fell.'

'What's *she* doing here?' Elise's eyes were fixed on Cassie.

'Cassie obviously heard the noise before you did.'

Cassie was amazed at his coolness, but Elise was openly disbelieving. Her eyes flashed fire while her hands worked furiously at her sides. 'That's impossible!' she hissed. 'Her room's at the other end of the house. She couldn't possibly have heard anything—unless of course she was in here already!'

It was plain that Elise had seen all there was to see, and though Cassie was shocked at her outburst, she could at least understand it. She opened her mouth to speak, but Ross silenced her with a look.

'You'd better leave us,' he said, and his fingers fastened round her arm, propelling her firmly towards the bathroom door. 'See what you can do in there.'

'Yes—get her out of here!' Elise spat. 'It's disgusting—she's like some kind of groupie! She should be sent back to the gutter, where she belongs——'

Cassie swung round at that, furious now. 'Ross!' she began, blazing, but Ross was already manoeuvring her through the door.

'In there,' he ordered curtly, 'and keep quiet!' And the door was slammed to behind her.

She stood in the darkened bathroom, chest heaving, and only slowly calming to the realisation that her feet were cold and wet. She fumbled for the light and stared blankly at the sodden carpet, but it didn't register. Her mind was still in the bedroom with Ross. What was he saying to Elise—and what was *she* saying to him? Shamelessly she turned and put her ear to the door, but all was quiet. He must have taken Elise back to her own room.

She let her breath out from between her teeth as her body relaxed against the door. Perhaps she, too, should go back to her own room? After all, Ross was going to have an awful lot of explaining to do. But, even though the thought was there, she didn't move. She pushed the hair off her face, her fingers sliding through the long tendrils in a weary movement.

For a moment back there it had almost seemed as though Elise didn't matter, as though nothing had mattered; nothing except the touch of their bodies and the look in his eyes. She had been on the point of surrender. She had let him caress her, she would have let him kiss her—she had *wanted* him to kiss her, and she had thought that he wanted it too. It had seemed as though the gulf between them had been swept away—that these last months had never happened, that they were in love

again. *In love!* Oh, God! She shook her head from side
to side, but she couldn't delude herself any longer. She
still loved him, she knew that now. The love that had
kept her grieving for him all this time, the love that she
thought had died on Saturday night—it had simply been
buried under the shock of realising that he was still alive,
that he hated her, and she had thought she hated him
too. But just now, in the bedroom, it had all come surging
back. She wanted him now as much as she had ever done.
She *loved* him now as much as she had ever done. She
closed her eyes in painful remembrance. If Elise hadn't
interrupted—Elise!

With a strangled sigh Cassie opened her eyes again.
There was no point in fooling herself. Nothing had happened—and, even if it had, no doubt afterwards Ross
would have been disgusted with himself—and with her.
It had simply been a moment's aberration on his part,
nothing more. After all, they had been close once, in
every possible way, and, whatever else his accident may
have done to him, Ross was still very much a man.
Perhaps it was just as well Elise had interrupted when
she had.

With a hiss of frustration Cassie pushed herself away
from the door. She'd better do something about the
carpet, she supposed. If it was left it would have shrunk
to the size of a postage stamp by morning. It was white,
too, which didn't help matters. A luxurious fluffy white
that exactly complemented the burgundy-coloured bath
and suite. There were mirrors, too, all along the back
wall, and her own reflection stared back at her: untidy,
dishevelled, two bright spots of colour in her cheeks,
and her dressing-gown clinging damply to her in places

from when she'd frantically wrung out that first towel to bathe Ross's burns.

She turned away from her reflection to pull yet another towel savagely off the rail, sinking to her knees and beginning to mop furiously at the carpet.

It was ironic, she thought, that just as she had realised how much she wanted to stay here, Ross would probably be intent on getting rid of her. After this he wouldn't want her within a hundred miles of The Breck. He would probably phone the garage himself first thing in the morning and pack her off as quickly as possible. But now she knew she *had* to stay. She sat back on her heels, picking bits of white fluff off the maroon towel.

She had to try and find some way of getting through to him. She couldn't tell him she still loved him, of course. He would never believe her, anyway. He didn't trust her—he would think it was another trick, and she had far too much pride to grovel. No, she would just have to wait, she realised desolately. Wait and hope that eventually he would come to his senses, begin to trust her again...but after Elise's insinuations the other night it might already be too late for that.

The door opened suddenly and Ross himself came in, closing the door behind him with a decisive click and leaning back on it. His face appeared white and set in the bright bathroom light, and the look in those narrowed, steely grey eyes sent a shiver of apprehension through her. The bathroom suddenly seemed very small and claustrophobic.

'Ross?' she began, but she got no further, for he reached down and hauled her to her feet, his fingers biting painfully into her upper arms.

'You're hurting me!' she gasped, but instead of releasing her he pulled her against him, so that her body was against his, her face only inches from his own.

'I wish I could break your damn neck!' he bit out.

'The carpet's ruined,' she gulped. 'I'm sorry—it was my fault——'

'Forget the bloody carpet!' He seemed to grind the words out from between his teeth. 'You think you're so damn clever, don't you? You think you know every trick in the book and you just can't resist playing with fire!'

'I don't know what you mean——'

'Oh, yes, you do, my girl! You know damn well what I mean, but this time you're not going to wriggle out of it so easily. It's about time you learned that you should always finish what you've started!'

And before she could react she was imprisoned against him, and his mouth had come down on hers in a fierce, hard kiss.

He was punishing her, she realised dazedly, and she tried to struggle, to protest, but she was clamped against him. Her mind was stunned, hardly capable of coherent thought, but the effect on the rest of her was immediate. The heat of his body against hers, the feel of him, was making her senses reel, her mind cloud with desire. There was a familiar ache beginning deep inside her, an ache she couldn't ignore, despite the small voice clamouring in her head. After all, hadn't she already admitted to herself that she was still in love with him? And didn't she want this just as much as he did?

For now his kiss was changing: no longer punishing, but demanding, seeking, and his body was throbbing and hardening against hers. Her arms slid up, almost of their own accord, to encircle his neck, and she arched

herself against him, hearing him groan deep in his throat
with increasing excitement. The ache in her loins was
now a burning need for fulfilment, invading every inch
of her, drowning every other thought in her head, and
when he lowered her on to the dry area of the fluffy
carpet she was incapable of resistance. His hands and
mouth were everywhere, stroking, fondling, almost as
though he couldn't get enough of her, and when his
mouth came back to hers she gave herself up completely
to its demanding, insidious sweetness...

CHAPTER FIVE

'Looks as if it'll clear up again later,' Dora announced, to no one in particular. She was staring out of the kitchen window while her hands swished busily in the sink, washing up the few remaining breakfast dishes. There was a dishwasher in the corner, but Cassie had only seen it working once. She sat at the table, pushing Dora's delicious cooked breakfast from one side of her plate to the other, and, while for the last two mornings she had cleared her plate, this morning she couldn't eat a thing.

She had woken alone in the big bed, only the aching languor of her body and a dent in the pillow next to hers to remind her of what had happened in the night. She had crept out of Ross's bed and along the passage to her own room, praying she would meet no one on the way.

It had been early, but she knew Dora and Willis would be up, and she had gone down for breakfast half expecting Ross to be there too, but when she descended the stairs to the hall it was to hear the busy clatter of the typewriter from behind the closed study door, and to have Dora announce unnecessarily that 'Mr Ross' was working.

So she still had the ordeal of facing him, and how could she know what his reaction was going to be? She prodded her egg with her fork. After the trauma of these last few days, the passions of last night seemed hardly credible, and there was a voice in her head, screaming at her for being a fool, for playing so easily into the trap he had so obviously set for her last night. And yet, had it been a trap? Lying with him in the warm darkness, she had thought she sensed something else...an indefinable something. The bitterness had gone, to be replaced by something far more potent...last night! Despite that small voice, a thrill of excitement leapt through her whenever she thought of last night. That warm, passionate body, that searching mouth...it was hard to believe that last night hadn't changed things, that this morning he wouldn't be pleased to see her...and yet there was still Elise.

She stared into her teacup, eyes shadowed. She didn't dare fool herself into thinking that last night had changed anything—except perhaps make it harder for her to leave; and that voice was there again. Perhaps that, too, was part of the plan, that terrible vendetta that Ross seemed intent on completing. Perhaps he *had* deliberately lured her to his room last night, with the specific intention of seducing her? Knowing that when he finally sent her away it would be the most perfect form of revenge—but she pushed these thoughts away. She couldn't believe that of him, not after last night. The tiny hope was growing that at long last he was beginning to believe her, that over these next few days she could perhaps prove to him...

'If you don't want it, just leave it.' Dora had turned and was watching her, sudsy hand on hip, and Cassie looked down guiltily at her plate.

'I'm sorry, Dora. I'm just not hungry this morning.'

'Hmmm...' Dora took the plate, lips pursed. 'That's what Mr Ross said earlier, but he didn't look like a whitewashed ghost. Seemed quite cheerful, in fact. Keen to get back to his writing, too, and he hasn't been near that typewriter of his for a fortnight as I know of.' She turned back to the sink, swishing the plate through the suds before setting it to drain. 'He said for you to go through as soon as you're ready.'

Cassie's head jerked up as her stomach suddenly plunged. 'He wants to see me?'

'Reckon he does.'

'Did he say what about?'

Dora flicked the tea-towel off the drainer to wipe her hands, lips pursed once more. 'No, he didn't, but he had a bad night again last night—you should have seen the state of his bathroom this morning, and Mrs Maxwell went in to see him first thing and came out with a face like thunder; so if I were you I wouldn't keep him waiting!'

All was silent as Cassie hesitated nervously by the closed study door. Perhaps he was going to send her away, after all? Dora had relayed the message as though it was some kind of dreadful summons—but perhaps that was just Dora.

She smoothed her palms over the hips of her jeans before knocking tentatively at the panels. There was no response, and she knocked again, louder, swallowing past the dry apprehension in her throat.

At a brief 'Come in' she slid round the door and stood just inside, hands thrust into the pockets of her jeans in what she hoped was a nonchalant manner. Inside she was shaking, but she mustn't let him see it. These last few days had taken their toll; she had to be prepared for anything, and until she knew what his reaction was going to be she had to appear cool and calm, giving nothing away.

Her eyes had moved immediately to where he stood by the window. He was using two sticks again this morning, and her gaze flicked over him in a quiver of alarm, but the hands that gripped the sticks showed no hint of strain, and his shoulders appeared broad and straight against the light. He was relatively formally dressed too, well-pressed cord trousers and a dark shirt under a fine woollen jumper, but he was silent, and she was too, waiting, watching for him to make the first move.

And then he said, 'Do you think you can handle a Bentley?'

'A Bentley?' This wasn't what she had expected at all. 'Well—I——'

'It's a much bigger car than you're used to, but the roads are pretty quiet at this time of year.'

He hadn't turned, hadn't even glanced at her, and her stomach plunged sickeningly. Was this it, then? Was he sending her away, after all? Had he shut himself off from her so completely that last night had meant absolutely nothing?

Her throat had closed up, and at her continued silence he turned, eyes narrowed to two dark, unreadable chasms as he looked at her.

'Ross——' she gulped, desperate now to do something—*anything*. 'Ross—about last night——'

'What about it?'

'Well—I—about what happened——'

'Do you expect me to apologise?'

'What? Oh—no——'

'Good. I had no intention of apologising, anyway. After all, I wanted it to happen——'

She stared at him. 'You did?'

'You did too, didn't you?' He was watching her, eyes still narrowed intently. She nodded dumbly.

'We're both consenting adults,' he murmured huskily, 'and two years is a long time...'

'Oh, Ross!' she breathed, a surge of emotion making her voice tremble, her body ache to be close to him, but still she stayed where she was, unsure, confused. 'Then— I don't understand,' she stammered. 'What was all that about a Bentley?'

He took a couple of steps towards her, mouth twisting upwards in a wry smile. 'It's my day for the hospital in Lancaster. Willis usually drives me, but he slipped on the cobbles in the yard last night, on his way back from the pub. He's sprained his ankle.'

It took a moment for his words to sink in, and when they did the effect was overwhelming, but there was no hint of what she was feeling in her voice when she said, 'You mean—he was *drunk*?'

It seemed impossible to imagine the stony-faced Willis as anything other than upright and sober and—stony-faced! Feeling as she did, she had to stifle a gurgle of almost hysterical amusement.

'The cobbles were wet.' Ross's voice, too, was expressionless, but the amusement in his eyes was undeniable, and she couldn't help but respond to it. They grinned at each other, and then they were laughing, spontaneous, uproarious laughter, and the tension between them was draining away.

After a moment Cassie sobered. She moved past him to stand where he had stood, by the window, hands still thrust into her jeans.

'What about Elise?' she said, her voice muffled. 'Wouldn't she rather take you into Lancaster?'

There was silence for a moment, and then he said, 'Elise isn't here.'

She swung round, hardly daring to believe her ears. 'You mean—she's *left*?' It seemed too good to be true, and she searched his face for any sign of anger, disappointment, regret—but his features were a mask behind which anything he may have felt was deftly hidden. Only his eyes were alive, and they were still fixed on her face in that intent stare.

'Well? Aren't you going to jump for joy? It was what you wanted, wasn't it? You made no secret of your dislike of her.'

She looked away. 'I never said I didn't like her.'

'You didn't have to.'

She sighed heavily. Although she wasn't looking at him, she was still vitally aware of him, of every brief nuance of expression in his voice, every slight shift of that lean body.

'I can't pretend I'm not glad she's gone,' she said at last. 'But no doubt you'll be seeing her again?'

It was half question, half statement of fact, and she hardly dared breathe, watching, waiting for his answer.

'No doubt I will.'

It was only what she'd expected, wasn't it? So why did she feel this stab of pain, this awful desolation? She turned back to the window, hands clenched in her pockets once more, throat aching with the effort of keeping silent.

He had come to stand behind her. She could feel his breath on her nape. Then suddenly he swung her round, fingers grasping her chin in a steely grip to tip her face up to his. He stared at her for a moment, the grey eyes narrowed, piercingly intent, as though he could see past her damp eyelids, her quivering mouth, through to her very soul.

'I'm making no promises, Cassie,' he said, his voice suddenly harsh, 'and I expect none from you. Promises are too easily broken. Understand?'

She swallowed, then nodded.

He stared at her for a moment longer, and for a second she thought he was going to add something else, but then suddenly she was released and he was moving to the door.

'My appointment is at eleven-thirty,' he said. 'We'll leave in half an hour.'

When she went outside the sun was shining, melting the clouds into fluffy balls of cotton wool that drifted harmlessly across the distant hills, their shadows trailing behind them; while on the cobbles stood an enormous Bentley, its paintwork gleaming despite its evident age. This was Uncle Nick's old car, kept in pristine condition by Willis. He was there too, flicking an imaginary speck of dust off the windscreen, and though his granite features were as impassive as ever, from his stiff, 'Good morning, miss,' Cassie realised he was far from pleased at having his pride and joy consigned to the care of a woman driver, especially one who had already wrapped her own car round the gatepost! But there was nothing she could do about that. The Land Rover, with its almost non-existent springs and hard seats, was obviously far from suitable for taking Ross all the way into Lancaster, while the springs of the Bentley were no doubt in excellent condition, as was the leather upholstery in its luxurious interior.

'Don't worry, Willis, I'll take good care of it,' Cassie murmured, as Willis held the driver's door open for her.

'I'm sure you will, miss,' he muttered reprovingly, and Cassie had to stifle a smile as he shut the door behind her with a decisive click and hobbled painfully round to the other side. Ross had just appeared, manoeuvring himself down the steps from the front of the house, and Willis helped him into the passenger seat, stowing the sticks carefully on the back seat, next to an enormous hamper.

'What's the hamper for?' Cassie asked, surprised.

'Lunch,' Ross replied, face impassive.

'Lunch? But I thought——'

'You thought we'd be back for lunch?' Ross was staring out of the windscreen, inspecting the rapidly disappearing clouds. 'By the time old Rogers at the hospital has finished with me it will be well past lunch time. I thought we'd stop for a picnic somewhere on the way back.'

His eyes had slid round to meet hers, devastatingly intent, and she felt her heart miss a beat. She turned to the front, reaching for the ignition, and a flood of excited anticipation washed over her.

The prospect of a picnic was a tempting one, and she tried to ignore the small voice in her head that cried, Fool! fool! Remember, he said no promises!

I don't care, she told herself fiercely. I don't care! She was with Ross, the old, smiling Ross, with the prospect of a whole day in his company, and she didn't want to question it, she didn't want to question anything, she just wanted to enjoy it, to enjoy the day, and she would face tomorrow when it came.

As Ross had said, the Bentley was a much bigger car
than she was used to. The roads were narrow and winding
and steeply graded in places, and for the first few miles
she had to concentrate on her driving, but Ross seemed
perfectly relaxed. He sat with his arm along the partly
open window of the car, pointing out places of interest,
farms and houses of families he knew, and occasionally
raising his hand to people they passed on the road; other
cars, and once some men working in a field.

He seemed to know almost everyone, Cassie realised,
and they him. Even though the homes in this area were
scattered and isolated, it didn't stop everyone knowing
their neighbours, and no doubt their business as well.
Unlike London, she mused, where she could walk from
one end of the square to the other and not meet a single
person she knew. No wonder Ross had wanted to keep
her at The Breck these last few days; if she had gone
wandering off on Saturday night no doubt the whole
district would have been buzzing with gossip by Sunday
morning.

'You're very quiet.' Ross had turned and was watching
her, the grey eyes slitted against the brightness outside.

'I was just thinking,' she admitted, 'you seem to know
almost everyone around here.'

'I ought to. I've lived here since I was twelve.'

'You've spent most of the last ten years in London,'
she pointed out, throwing him a quick glance, and he
turned back to viewing the passing countryside, face
impassive.

'My uncle's family have lived in this area for generations. Uncle Nick was well liked. As his adopted son,
I've inherited some of his glory.'

'You never talked about him much,' she ventured. 'I never realised how close you were.'

'He was the father I never had.'

She threw him a quick, searching glance. 'Is that why you used his name for your book?'

'I wanted to go some way towards repaying him,' he said simply.

She digested this in silence for a moment, and then, voice carefully controlled, she began, 'Elise told me he was something of a recluse. Was that because of—what happened?'

'The Breck was all he had left,' Ross declared. 'His only worry was that he no longer had the money to keep it in good repair.'

'So that's why you're doing it up now,' she murmured, and felt his eyes on her face again.

'It's my home,' he stated flatly. 'Is there anything wrong with that?'

'No,' she replied, eyes straight to the front, fixed on the road again. 'Nothing wrong with it at all.' If anything, it was a sign of just how much he cared, she thought hollowly. If only she could be as certain of his feelings towards *her*.

They were approaching the crest of a hill, nothing but blue sky visible beyond it, but as they rounded the gentle bend and began to descend Cassie's breath caught in her throat.

The whole panorama of Morecambe Bay was spread out below them. To the left, the flat green fields of the Fylde; to the right, a narrow strip of coastline stretching away to Grange-over-Sands and Barrow, and, rising behind it, just visible in the haze, the peaks of the Lake District; while between them both the sea shimmered and sparkled in an expanse of blue-green that stretched away to the horizon.

They descended the hill and they were in Lancaster.

'What are you going to do with yourself for the next couple of hours?' Ross asked, and she stared at him in surprise.

'Don't you need me?'

'No. There's a good museum here—Lancaster is built on the site of an old Roman fort—or there's the castle. The Lancashire Witches were sent for trial and hanged there.'

She shuddered. 'No, thanks. I'll probably look round the shops.' But when she'd dropped Ross off and found somewhere to park the car, instead of heading towards the shops, she walked down to the river where she sat for a while, hands thrust into her pockets and coat buttoned up against the stiff breeze off the sea. She found herself thinking longingly of the hamper on the back seat of the car and realised she was hungry—she'd eaten hardly any breakfast. So she set off walking again, this time to find a café, where she settled herself in a window-seat, staring absently out at the passers-by while she sipped her coffee and munched her way through home-made scones and jam. Someone had left a newspaper on the seat opposite and she scanned the headlines with detached interest. She hadn't seen a newspaper since she'd been at The Breck, although she knew Willis usually picked up several dailies for Ross every morning. She flicked idly over the inside pages and then suddenly stopped and turned hurriedly back as a photograph caught her eye—and she was staring at the granite features of her grandfather.

She read the accompanying paragraph with a quickening heart, but it merely commented on his sudden illness and the fact that he was now out of intensive care and progressing steadily. It didn't tell her anything she didn't already know, but her eyes returned to the photograph, staring at it fixedly, a heavy frown between her brows.

She arrived back at the hospital to find Ross already waiting. She reached across to open the passenger door for him, and then took the sticks while he settled himself in the seat.

'Have you been waiting long?' she murmured.

'Only about five minutes. I saw you come round the corner.'

She was watching him, studying his face thoughtfully. 'You seem very cheerful about it.'

'I don't have to come back for another six weeks. Old Rogers seems amazed by my sudden progress.' He turned to grin at her, eyes mockingly intent, but she looked away, fiddling with the gears, and accelerated away without a word.

Back in the hills, he directed her to a sheltered spot he knew of, and they settled themselves by the side of a small, stony beck, half hidden from the road by a bank of bracken and heather. Dora had packed a delicious array of food, more than enough for the two of them, but, after nibbling her way through a couple of sandwiches, Cassie found she had had enough. Her appetite of an hour ago seemed to have completely deserted her, and she lay back against the bank, eyes closing automatically against the glare of blue above her.

The sun was warm on her face, the grass cushioned her back, and the only sounds were the birds and the breeze in the pines far above their heads and the gurgling beck at their feet; and yet Cassie was in no mood to appreciate it. Instead, she found her thoughts returning again and again to that article she'd read about her grandfather. The photograph had been an old one, taken about ten years ago, and when she remembered how he had looked on Friday night, when she had visited him last, there was no comparison. And yet the doctors were reasonably confident now that he would make a good recovery. Despite the severity of his attack, he had been reasonably lucky. He would be in a wheelchair for a while, yes, but he could still speak, he could still use his limbs. So why couldn't she shake off the sudden doubts that seeing that article seemed to have planted in her mind?

Something brushed her face and she opened her eyes. Ross lay propped on one elbow next to her, trailing a stalk of feathery grass across her cheek.

He smiled a wry, crooked smile. 'Sleepyhead.'

She managed a smile in return, and then his shadow fell across her as his mouth came down to hers, lightly caressing, and trailed tantalisingly across her cheek to her throat, before moving back to the corner of her mouth.

'Your face is red,' he murmured.

'So is yours.' She looked up into those grey eyes, so close to her own. How did Ross feel about her grandfather's heart attack? Did he know how it had affected him—all of them?

His mouth came down again, more insistent this time, soft and warm, sweetly tempting, and she felt her body beginning its own unconscious response. But her mind remained obstinately, persistently clear. She couldn't rid herself of her grandfather's face; it was there every time she closed her eyes.

After a moment Ross raised his head, his eyes narrowed, and she sighed, unconsciously turning her head away from him. Suddenly, everything had changed.

'You haven't eaten much,' Ross said at last, and the change in him, too, seemed almost a tangible thing. 'Dora won't be very pleased.'

She sighed again and fiddled absently with a stalk of grass, reluctant to speak. All day she had avoided any mention of the past, and it seemed he had, too, but it was there between them all the same. It had simply been buried for a few hours under passions and longings they had been unable to control. But seeing that article had brought it all back, and already it was beginning to eat away at this precarious new intimacy that seemed to have sprung up between them. She could keep it inside her no longer.

'I was thinking about my grandfather,' she said at last.

There was a silence. She felt, rather than saw him lie back against the bank again, face to the sky.

'I know how loyal you are, Cassie, to your family at least—even though I consider that loyalty to be somewhat misplaced where they're concerned—but believe me, your grandfather is a tough old bird. He can take care of himself.'

'I used to think so, but now I'm not so sure.' She bit her lip, hesitating, before throwing him a quick glance. 'He dreads the thought of retirement.'

'It'll have to come sooner or later.'

'Brett's is his life.'

'Men like that never give up completely.'

'I've heard the family talking,' she got out. 'They'll try to pressurise him.'

'Have you ever known him to bow to pressure before—unless it was in his own interests?' Ross's voice had become colder, harder. 'Anyhow, he can handle it. He's known for years that James covets his position—and Elaine covets it even more! She can hardly wait for James to step into his father's shoes.'

The bitterness in his voice was unmistakable and Cassie turned her head to stare at him, but she didn't contradict him. How could she, when she knew that the gist of what he said was true? Elaine had always been ambitious above everything else. She stared miserably up at the sky.

'You know there's going to be an inquiry into allegations of malpractice at Brett's?' she said now, and it was an effort to keep her voice level.

'Yes.'

She turned to stare at him again, but his eyes were narrowed to two unfathomable slits against the glare of the sun. She opened her mouth to speak but he raised his arm, glancing at his watch, effectively cutting off anything she might have been about to say.

'It's time we were getting back,' he stated harshly, and reached for his sticks.

Ross was silent on the way back, and Cassie was too. The day had gone horribly flat, she thought miserably. The promise of this morning was falling round her in glittering fragments. But then this morning she had been deluding herself into thinking that last night had changed things, and she could see now that it hadn't changed anything—except perhaps to prove that she and Ross were still physically attracted to each other. But that was all it could be now, physical attraction. There were too many other things between them, unanswered questions, things she herself still didn't understand.

As if to mirror her growing depression the sun, too, was disappearing, hidden behind great black clouds that were advancing relentlessly from the north, and as they pulled on to the cobbles the first raindrops began to splatter against the windscreen. By the time they sat down to dinner it was raining heavily, a steady downpour that had obviously set in for the night, and the sound of the rain outside seemed to contrast starkly with the lack of conversation inside. Ross seemed—preoccupied, and Cassie wondered vaguely whether today had been too much for him, he was frowning almost as though he was in pain. But she didn't voice her thoughts. The intimacy of this morning seemed to have completely disappeared.

Once Dora had served their coffee and left them to themselves in the sitting-room, the silence seemed to stretch between them unbearably. Ross sat in his usual armchair by the fire, legs stretched out to the blaze, eyes fixed on the flames in a black frown; but Cassie couldn't settle, she stood by the window, staring out at the sodden lawn and damp, dripping trees. Fear was gnawing at her, the fear that she could no longer put off what she knew now was inevitable. Questions were burning in her mind and she had to find some answers—no matter what the consequences might be.

There was a glass-fronted cabinet to one side of the window with some framed photographs arranged on top of it. A couple were of Ross, and one was of a man and woman she assumed were his parents, but there was another one, of an older man, seated behind a desk and

smiling into the camera. She picked it up and studied it
for a moment before holding it out to Ross. 'Is this your
uncle—Nicholas Daleford?'

His eyes moved round to hers, dark and intense. 'Yes.'

'Did you take it?'

He nodded. 'He had an office overlooking Piccadilly.
When I was still at school I used to meet him there
sometimes and he'd take me out for lunch in Manchester.
That camera was a birthday present. That was one of
the first pictures I ever took with it.'

'So you were quite old when—when your uncle went
out of business?'

'I was seventeen. Old enough to know what it was all
about, but too young to do anything about it—but what
has that got to do with anything?' His eyes were still
fixed on her face, searching, probing. 'You could only
have been about eight. You weren't even a Brett then,
were you? Or is there something you know and I don't?'

Cassie had her back to him as she put the photograph
back on the cabinet. She'd been about eight when her
father had left home and James Brett had begun to call
regularly on her mother.

'Did you know any of the people who worked for your
uncle?' she asked hollowly.

'No. I only wish I had.'

She turned back to face him, her own eyes dark now,
and intensely green. 'There was an inquiry, wasn't there,
when the designs disappeared?'

'There should have been an inquiry when Brett's came
up with an almost identical design!'

'It could have been coincidence——'

'It could have been, yes. It could have been coincidence, too, that my uncle was a friend of your grand-

father's, a friend who was conveniently dropped as soon as it was realised he was going out of business!'

Her eyes jerked back to his face. 'I didn't know that.'

'No, I don't suppose you did. Alexander Brett wouldn't advertise the fact, would he? And he was always careful enough to keep out of my way when I was with you.'

She stared at him, her face full of searching uncertainty as her eyes traced the lines of bitter pain in those harshly set features. 'Is that why you wrote those articles, Ross? Because of what you thought Brett's had done to your uncle—because of what you thought *I'd* done to *you*?'

'My uncle had nothing to do with those articles,' he bit out.

'But you used the story to get into Brett's—to get inside information,' she accused tonelessly. 'And while we're on the subject, where did that information come from exactly?'

His eyes were still on her face. 'I think that's obvious.'

'Me?' She shook her head slowly from side to side. 'No, Ross, I know it wasn't me, and if you try to tell me it was then I'll know you're shielding someone else.'

'You can't be sure of that.'

'I'm as sure as I can be about anything,' she replied determinedly. 'Admittedly, at first I thought it was me, yes, but when I sat down and thought about it I realised that if you'd wanted information I was the last person you'd come to. I'm the one member of the family who's had hardly any involvement in Brett's.'

'Your family are immersed in the business,' he retorted coolly. 'You let out more than you knew.'

'Did I? I don't think so. I can't recall even discussing Brett's with you above half a dozen times, and certainly not in any detail; besides, you never asked me. You were always more interested in—other things.'

'You never complained,' he interrupted tautly. 'You were as eager as me!' His face was hardening now, his eyes cooling to two chips of ice, but she would not be put off.

'All those afternoons at your flat,' she continued hollowly. 'There was always stuff lying about: books, papers, half-written articles; you never hid anything away, but I never saw anything even remotely connected with Brett's—and yet Bill Hodges told me you were working on those articles before the accident. That means you already had the information, that you were carrying it round with you in your head. Why didn't you use it then, Ross? Why wait? *Why——?*'

'All right—*all right*!' Ross swung himself out of the chair to limp across to the hearth. 'You want to hear me say it? It was because of *us*, Cassie! Because we were together, because of what we meant to each other—or rather, what *you* meant to *me*!'

She stared at him. 'And afterwards?' she got out.

'It's my job. My editor was pressing me for the story.'

'And you're telling me that's the only reason?'

His eyes had narrowed, glacier-like now in their intensity. 'You're doubting my ethics as a journalist? That's a very serious charge, Cassie, and one I don't take too kindly to, not from you.'

'You've already told me Bill Hodges has refused to accept any more articles because of your "emotional involvement",' she pointed out, and it was an effort to meet his look, to keep her gaze steady under that fierce glare.

'Are you accusing me of deliberately defaming Brett's for personal motive?' he grated. 'Libel is a dangerous word, Cassie, you should be careful what you say!'

Her eyes were steady, intensely green. 'Do you really believe James and Grandfather Brett were fiddling contracts?'

'It's not a question of what I believe! I simply present the facts——'

'But facts can be presented in many different ways, Ross, as we both know to our cost!' She thrust her hands into the pockets of her jeans. 'You told me on Saturday night that you'd do anything you could to bring me down——'

'And you really believe I'd jeopardise my career—everything I've worked for—just to get back at you and your family?' His eyes were still narrowed dangerously and she turned away, running her fingers through her hair, unable to sustain his look any longer.

'I don't know what to believe!' she got out. 'At one time I would never have believed it of you, Ross, no. I trusted you, I thought I knew you—I *loved* you, Ross. But now—everything's changed, *you've* changed——'

She faltered, but he continued bitingly, 'And now you're not so sure, eh? You can't be certain whether my reasons were purely altruistic or buried under a mass of—what did you call it? *Self-pity!* My God—do you think I don't know where all this is leading?' he exclaimed bitterly. 'All that talk of your grandfather this afternoon—you're accusing me of being directly responsible for his heart attack!'

She turned back to him. 'I didn't say that——' she began.

'But that was what you meant, wasn't it?' he demanded harshly.

She shook her head, as much to clear her mind as in denial. Was that what she was saying—or was he putting words into her mouth? She couldn't be sure. Put directly like that, it sounded so ugly, and yet she couldn't shake off her suspicions.

'I don't know——' she began.

'Don't you?' he bit out. 'I do. Was it a deliberate act, or simply pure coincidence? You can't be sure—and neither can I! It's something we'll never know for certain now, will we?' He was limping towards the drinks cabinet, reaching into the cupboard for a glass and slamming the cupboard door to again with controlled violence. 'What it all boils down to, Cassie, is trust,' he continued harshly. 'And that's something we don't have, do we? You don't trust me—and I don't trust you. So we're back to where we started—stalemate!'

He poured himself a whisky and she watched him, unable to speak for the tightness in her throat. His words seemed to be ringing a death knell in her heart, and after a moment she turned back to the window, hands clenched in her pockets, staring unseeingly out at the rain. A terrible coldness was enveloping her.

'I—I think I'd better phone the garage in the morning——' she began, 'to see if my car's ready...'

She waited for him to speak, but he was silent.

'Perhaps it would be better if I went back to London...'

'As you wish.' His voice was expressionless now and she turned back to face him, eyes huge and overbright with unshed tears, lips pressed together in a trembling line.

'So that's it, then,' she got out at last. 'That's all you can say?'

He was staring into his glass, face clenched into a taut mask. 'What do you want me to say? I thought we'd agreed this morning—no promises!'

'*We* agreed?' she burst out tremulously. 'You mean *you* agreed, it was your idea! No promises—what you really meant was no commitments!'

'Promises—commitments—what does it matter? They're all the same. Perhaps that was where I went wrong last time—I expected too much——'

'Ross—*Ross!*' The awful finality in his voice was tearing her to pieces. 'What—what if I told you I didn't want to leave, that I wanted to stay here—with you—under *any* circumstances, Ross? You said yourself—we meant something to each other once——'

She had thrown in her last desperate card and she watched his face, willing him to look at her, give her a sign—anything, but he was staring into his glass, swirling the liquid round with intense concentration.

'At the beginning of the week you couldn't wait to get away,' he said at last, and his voice was low, hoarse. 'Well, now I'm giving you your freedom. You're free to leave whenever you wish.'

She stood like a statue, staring at him. 'And you'll let me go?' she whispered. 'Just like that?'

'What did you expect? That I'd crawl on my knees and beg you to stay?' The look on his face made her wince. 'And if you did stay, how long would it be before you left me again? A day? A week? A month?' He banged his glass down and limped tautly back to the

hearth again. 'I've told you, Cassie, there's no trust between us. How can we possibly have anything else
without that?'

Her heart seemed to have shrivelled and died inside
her. Only her tears were alive, warm and damp, rolling
unchecked down her cheeks. The rest of her was cold
emptiness. She turned away, back to the window, seeing
nothing but the blur of tears.

'You're still absolutely convinced that I walked out
on you, aren't you?' she got out, and she heard him
swear.

'My God, you're not going to begin another denial,
Cassie, not *now*?'

'There's no point, is there?' Her voice was a cracked
facsimile of itself. 'But I'd like you to remember that—
that *I* was in hospital too. I was unconscious for nearly
two days, and then I was moved away—to a private
clinic——'

'I know.'

She swung round, glaring at him through her tears.
'*How* do you know?' she accused. 'How can you *possibly* know?'

'You know damn well how I know!' He pushed his
fingers through his hair in a quick, tense movement, and
she saw a muscle jerk in his cheek.

'No, I don't,' she cried. '*Tell* me.'

'My God!' he ejaculated hoarsely. 'You really want
your pound of flesh, don't you?' He took a harsh breath
and swung back to the hearth, leaning with his fists on
the mantelpiece. And then, 'It was Elaine.'

She stared at him uncomprehendingly. 'Elaine? My
mother?'

He gave a travesty of a smile. 'The very same! She came to see me—remember? You sent her to tell me you never wanted to see me again!'

CHAPTER SIX

EVERY mile that took Cassie further from The Breck seemed to ring a death knell in her heart, but there was only one thought burning in her head now. She had to get back to London, to see Elaine, to see for herself if there was the slightest grain of truth in this latest horrendous accusation and her own dreadful suspicions.

She had left at first light this morning, with only a worried-looking Dora to see her off, fretting that she was in no state to drive all the way to London, that she should at least wait and see Mr Ross...but what would be the point of that? Everything had been said. She had walked out of the sitting-room last night and out of his life, and there was no way she could go back.

She put her foot on the accelerator and pulled out to overtake a lorry, flicking the windscreen wipers on against the spray off his tyres. Then there was the steady click-click of the indicator as she pulled in again and settled back in her lane. It was still raining.

There was something else that disturbed her, something she had only discovered this morning. The garage had informed The Breck yesterday morning that her car was ready. Willis had arranged to pick it up, and yet Ross had never told her. He had kept her at The Breck, persuaded her to drive him into Lancaster, to spend the afternoon with him...the speedometer needle was hovering in the nineties and she took a breath, easing her foot off the accelerator, taking her hands off the wheel one at a time to wipe her palms on her skirt, forcing herself to relax.

Perhaps Dora was right. She wasn't in any state to drive down to London today—not on the motorway, anyway. But she would get there. She had to, to see Elaine.

And yet, if she were to have an accident on the way— say her car ran off the road and she was killed—it would save everyone a lot of hassle, wouldn't it? Hadn't she already accepted that there was nothing for her with Ross? And in some ways that made the pain more unbearable than it had been when she had simply believed he was dead...

The car swerved suddenly and her hands automatically tightened on the steering wheel, steadying it again. No, she had no intention of dying yet. At least, not until after she had seen Elaine...

London seemed like another planet. She drove straight to James's house and parked, letting herself in with her key without even waiting for Nancy to open the door. The housekeeper was hurrying down the stairs and her face broke into a relieved smile when she saw who it was.

'My dear—thank goodness you're back! The family were worried——'

'Where's my mother?' Cassie interrupted without preamble.

Nancy looked taken aback. 'Well—I—in the sitting-room, I imagine——' she began, but Cassie was already striding purposefully towards the sitting-room door, hesitating only a fraction before thrusting it open.

Her mother stood by the french windows, a handkerchief twisted in her fingers, an untouched tray of tea on the little table by her side and to Cassie it seemed almost as though she had been expecting her.

'So you've come back at last!' Elaine exclaimed. Her voice sounded high-pitched, strained, and Cassie gazed at her mutely for a moment before closing the door behind her and leaning back on it.

'I've only been away four days, Mummy,' she said, and was surprised to hear how calm her own voice sounded in comparison.

'Four days?' Elaine burst out. 'It could have been four weeks! Don't you know James and I have been out of our minds with worry? You've never done anything like this before! For all we knew you could have been—have been——'

'Dead?' Cassie supplied coolly. 'I did phone you.'

'One brief phone call on Monday that told us absolutely nothing!' Elaine exclaimed petulantly. 'Honestly, Cassie, I'm beginning to think I don't understand you at all——'

'But then, you never have, have you?' Cassie interrupted, and Elaine's eyes jerked to her face in a sharp look.

'What's got into you, Cassie? Have you nothing to say—no apologies for all the worry you've put us through?'

'Don't you want to know where I've been?' Cassie returned in a low voice.

'Of course I do! You should know——'

'Can't you guess?'

'Of course I can't! You gave us no indication——'

'I've been with Ross.'

Elaine's furious outburst came to an abrupt halt. The sudden silence was electric. Cassie watched her mother's face, and Elaine stared back, almost as though she couldn't believe her ears.

'You've been—with Ross?'

'That's what I said.'

Elaine seemed to pull herself together. 'Now you're being ridiculous, Cassie. This is some kind of joke——'

'It's no joke.'

'Then what do you mean by it?' Elaine demanded shrilly. 'You burst in here, no explanations, just some enigmatic response about having "been with Ross"! You always were too much like your father——'

'I've been with Ross in Lancashire,' Cassie interrupted tightly. 'He isn't dead. But then, you knew that, didn't you?'

Elaine seemed to pale. 'What do you mean—I knew? How could I possibly know——'

'You went to see him. You knew he had survived the accident, but you let me go on believing it all this time——'

'Don't be ridiculous, Cassie!' Elaine remonstrated tremulously. 'That's a terrible accusation——'

'Yes, it is, isn't it? That's what I said to Ross, "that's a terrible accusation", but you haven't denied it, have you? That's because you *can't* deny it! You knew he was alive, didn't you? *Didn't you?*'

Elaine swung away, turned back to the window, staring out while her hands worked frantically on the handkerchief, clenching and unclenching. Then slowly she turned back to face Cassie, her hand on the back of the armchair, as though for support.

'Yes,' she whispered. 'I knew. My God—I knew it would all come out in the end——'

Cassie stood rigid, staring at her, feeling the blood draining from her face, almost, it seemed, the very life draining from her body, then her hands came up to cover her face and she turned into the door as the tears began their slow, immutable course. *So it was true!* She hadn't wanted to believe it, she hadn't *dared* believe it. She would rather it had been another of Ross's insane accusations...

'Why?' she choked. 'Why? *Why?*'

'Why?' Elaine echoed. 'The reasons why seem hardly to matter now, do they?' There was no denying the emotion in her voice. 'I thought I was saving you a lot of pain and misery——'

'*Pain* and *misery*?' Something inside Cassie seemed to snap. She swung round, face contorted, eyes burning through her tears. 'What do you think I'm feeling now if it isn't *pain* and *misery*?'

'You must understand——' Elaine's fingers worked convulsively, almost tearing the handkerchief to shreds. 'The doctors—everyone—had given up hope! His legs were crushed, he had spinal injuries—there was even talk of brain damage at one point! But you would have married him—you would have spent the rest of your life tied to a vegetable——'

'So you told me he was already dead!' Cassie accused hoarsely.

'No—*no!*' Elaine took a couple of frantic paces across the room. 'You don't understand! Cassie—you were already half convinced he couldn't possibly have survived!' She took a breath, obviously struggling for control. 'Cassie—the police told us that when they arrived at the scene of the accident you were still conscious. You were holding his hand and mumbling deliriously—you already knew how badly he was injured! Later, when you regained consciousness, you were already afraid he was dead——'

'So you simply kept quiet!' Cassie's face mirrored her disgust. She had never felt such furious, bitter anger. She thought she had remembered it all so clearly, but now, looking back, hearing Elaine's version of events, she realised her mind had been clouded with shock. During those first few days she had only been half aware of other people—of what was happening to her. It must have been easy for Elaine.

'What about Ross?' she demanded shakily. 'You couldn't keep quiet with him, could you? You had to go and see him!'

Elaine sank back into the armchair, nodding weakly. Her face appeared almost grey.

'He—he was asking for you all the time. At first he thought *you'd* died, but of course the doctors knew you hadn't—so I had to go and see him——' She faltered. 'I—I told him——'

'You told him I never wanted to see him again,' Cassie accused bitterly. 'Oh, God!' She collapsed weakly back against the door, closing her eyes against the awful knowledge of what that visit had done to Ross.

'How could you?' she whispered tautly. 'How *could* you?'

'I thought it was for the best,' Elaine cried, a sob in her voice. 'I did it for you, Cassie.'

'For *me*? And what about Neil—wasn't it for him, too?' Cassie accused hoarsely. 'Wasn't he in on this—and the rest of my beloved family?'

Elaine seemed to have aged twenty years. 'No—believe me—they knew nothing. James and Neil were away if you remember, and by the time they got back you'd already been moved into that private clinic——'

'So once again you kept quiet—my God, it must have seemed like a godsend! No nurses to ask questions—no doctors to drop subtle hints—and afterwards I was packed off to Aunt Vinny in Ireland. All very convenient and well thought out! And what then—or can I guess? Back to Neil—marriage—a house in the country——'

'And what's wrong with that?' Elaine burst out tremulously. 'You cared for him before—why not again? He could have given you security——'

'And babies to inherit Brett's Engineering!' Cassie retorted bitterly. 'And that's the point of all this, isn't it? Brett's! If I married Neil it would tie the family firm up very nicely for the next two generations!' She remembered Ross's words with bitter humour. 'It's ironic that if it hadn't been for grandfather's heart attack I would never have known anything about it—I probably would have married Neil in time, had his babies—and ended up bored and frustrated, just like Julia——'

'*Cassie!*'

'You engineered Julia's marriage,' Cassie continued wildly, 'and now you're trying to do the same with me! Well, I won't have it, do you understand? *I won't have it!*'

Some detached part of her brain was telling her she was becoming hysterical, and she took a breath, trying to steady herself and failing miserably. A terrible weariness was enveloping her, seeping into her brain, her limbs, and she collapsed against the door, clutching the handle for support, her face streaked with tears.

'Cassie—Cassie, you don't know what you're saying!' Elaine had sprung up from the chair and taken a step towards her. 'You make it sound as though I deliberately set out to hurt you—I'm your *mother*! Do you think I'd deliberately do anything to harm you? All this—it's been too much for you! You're still not over the shock of hearing about your grandfather—it's turned your mind!'

Cassie straightened away from the door, wiping her wet cheeks with unsteady fingers. 'Yes—perhaps you're right,' she got out in a low, fierce voice. 'It *has* turned my mind—but hearing about Grandfather Brett was only the beginning! You see—I saw Ross that first night at the hospital.' And at Elaine's look of shocked surprise, 'Oh, yes, I was convinced I was off my head! So later, when you mentioned Bill Hodges, I decided to go and see him.'

'My God—I knew, *I knew*!' Elaine passed a shaking hand over her eyes. 'The look on your face when I mentioned his name—I *knew* something was wrong. And then on Monday Natalie Peers phoned me, wanting to know why you weren't at the boutique. It came out that you'd been to see Bill Hodges, and she was worried; she said you seemed very—strange. I was afraid then that you'd discover the truth.' Elaine dabbed at her face and walked slowly back to the window. 'I was afraid Bill Hodges knew something about it, and that was why he was publishing those articles.'

'It was Ross who wrote those articles.'

There was a stunned silence. Elaine swung round.

'*Ross* wrote those articles?'

Cassie smiled hollowly. 'Don't you think it's strange, Mummy. how often in life events come round full circle?

You know *why* Ross wrote those articles—why he's been snooping round Brett's all this time? And now I think I should warn you we're getting down to the *real* reasons for this whole sordid mess—discovering the person who would gain the most from Ross's disappearance from my life! He wrote those articles to try and get back at Brett's for something that happened in Manchester almost fifteen years ago!'

'Manchester——?' Elaine echoed, and now her eyes were narrowed, fixed on Cassie's face in piercing intensity. 'What has Manchester go to do with this?'

'You were a secretary, weren't you, Mummy? A secretary in an engineering firm in Manchester? Tell me—what was your boss's name? Daleford? Nicholas Daleford?'

'Yes, I worked for Nicholas Daleford.' Elaine's eyes had widened. 'But you were far too young——'

'Some designs went missing,' Cassie got out. 'The firm went bust.'

There was a silence. Elaine's features were rigid, her eyes still round and staring, but now her gaze was blank with shock.

'I suppose you finally put two and two together,' she said at last.

'Why did you do it, Mummy?' Cassie asked bitingly. '*Why?* Was it for James? Did you get the designs for him? Did he *know* where they came from?'

'I suppose you told Ross?'

'No, I didn't tell him.' Cassie's mouth twisted grimly. 'How could I tell him that it was my own mother who betrayed his uncle? Besides, I only knew for certain myself last night. Tell me,' she bit out, 'did you love

James so much? Were you so desperate to get away from Daddy?'

Elaine had turned back to the window, staring unseeingly out. 'I had an affair with James,' she began simply. 'I knew that under other circumstances he would have brought me back to London with him, but I was married—and with two young children into the bargain—and a man of James's class——' She stopped, letting her breath out on a long, harsh sigh. 'It was a risk, but I was playing for high stakes. I knew that with a little effort I could get James to propose. And it was so easy—no one ever knew. Even at the inquiry no one suspected me.'

'And James?' Cassie demanded to know. 'What about him? Are you telling me that he didn't know either?'

Elaine gave a travesty of a smile. 'They say love is blind, Cassie, and I've certainly found it to be true! Your father—James—even you! You couldn't see what Ross Tyler was trying to do to you—to all of us! You see now why I disliked him from the first——'

'You knew he was Nicholas Daleford's nephew,' Cassie accused, and Elaine nodded, that taut little smile appearing and disappearing again.

'Yes, I knew. Of course, he didn't know me, but I recognised him from when he used to come to the office in Manchester. Mr Daleford used to talk about him a lot. I realised straight away why he was trying to worm his way into Brett's, but you were blind, weren't you, Cassie? You couldn't see that he was simply using you for information, and you gave it to him. You gave him everything he asked for——'

She stopped as Cassie slowly began to shake her head.

'Oh, no, Mummy, it wasn't me who gave Ross that information. You've accused me too many times of taking no interest in Brett's to know that it couldn't possibly have been me.'

Elaine was staring at her, and Cassie stared back, her gaze unflinching, and slowly Elaine staggered back into the armchair.

'Oh, my God!' she gasped. 'Then it must have been——'

Cassie's eyes narrowed. 'You know who it is?' she demanded.

Elaine was muttering almost incoherently. 'If it wasn't you, then there's only one other person it could have been, but Julia would never—she couldn't——'

'Julia?' Cassie echoed sharply.

Abruptly Elaine pulled herself out of the chair again to pace restlessly back and forth, hands clenched tightly together in front of her, her features pale and set.

'I didn't want to have to tell you this, Cassie, but now it seems I have no choice——'

'Tell me what?' Cassie automatically stiffened, bracing herself against what she dreaded was to come. And yet nothing could be as bad as what she knew already, could it? And if it concerned Ross, then she had to know...

'You remember where you first met Ross?' Elaine asked now, and Cassie gave a quick, impatient nod.

'Of course. I met him at one of Julia's parties.'

'Didn't you ever wonder what he was doing there? How he'd come to be invited? After all, Julia knows how I feel about journalists——'

Cassie moved her shoulders. 'I just assumed he was a friend of Julia's.'

'And you accepted that? You never questioned him about it?'

'No—why should I?' Cassie asked abruptly. That feeling of dread was growing.

Elaine seemed to hesitate, then she stated baldly, 'Julia was having an affair with him.'

'What?'

'You know how Julia is with—men,' Elaine continued tautly. 'Well, she'd been introduced to him somewhere or other—and she fell for him straight away. I realised immediately what a dangerous situation it could be and I tried to talk her out of it, but, of course, she wouldn't listen—you know how Julia is. Anyway, Ross had more brains than I gave him credit for. He played it cool, pretended he wasn't interested, and after a while Julia began to get desperate. She must have realised that information on Brett's was what he really wanted and started using it as bait—I remember going to meet James one day and finding her sat behind Roddy's desk, going through his drawers. I remember thinking at the time how guilty she looked, but I didn't think any more of it, and now—it all seems to fall into place——'

Elaine's voice trailed away, but Cassie could only stare at her, white-faced. Then she asked tonelessly, 'And what about me? Where did I fit into all this?'

'Julia had suspected for some time that there must be someone else,' Elaine continued slowly, 'but, of course, we didn't realise who it was, not until it was too late——'

'I see.'

Elaine was watching her uncertainly. 'Cassie—darling—is that all you can say?'

'What else is there to say?' Cassie turned, her hand on the doorknob. She felt suddenly, curiously detached, and all she wanted to do now was get away—away from her mother, away from this house, away from everything.

'But Cassie—surely you're not going back to him?' Elaine demanded tremulously. 'After all that's happened—my God, you see now why I hated him—he was out to destroy us from the very first! He's deceived all of us—playing us off one against the other——'

'No, I'm not going back to him.'

Elaine was silenced, staring at her, and Cassie gave a travesty of a smile. 'You think I've come all this way just to confront you, Mummy? The greatest irony of all is that your plans have achieved their desired objective, after all! Everything has been destroyed, as effectively as if Ross *had* died in that accident, and I'm going to have to live with that for the rest of my life. Can you understand that, Mummy?' And as she turned and walked blindly out of the door and across the hall those words seemed to echo bleakly in her head. For the rest of my life. For the rest of my life... *For the rest of my life*...

Someone was shaking her. She opened her eyes and blinked up into the pale oval of Natalie's anxious features.

'Cassie—Cassie, wake up! Neil's here—he wants to see you. He says it's important! Apparently he's driven down from Lancashire. Cassie—he's got some garbled story about having seen Ross!'

'Ross?' Cassie sat up. She was still fully dressed, apart from her shoes, and her memory of the drive from

James's house to the flat she shared with Natalie was a complete blank.

'Cassie—Cassie, do you understand?' Natalie was shaking her again.

Cassie nodded dumbly and struggled to get off the bed. She padded round to where her shoes lay and slipped her feet into them, catching sight of herself in the mirror as she did so. In the darkness of the bedroom, with only the light from the hall for illumination, her eyes appeared dark and sunken, the bones of her face stood out starkly under her white skin, and her hair... She looked like a wild woman, she thought dully, but somehow it didn't seem to matter.

Neil was obviously shocked when he saw her. 'Cassie— good God!' he exclaimed, and helped her across to the armchair. When she was safely settled he turned away, pushing his fingers through his hair, obviously agitated, and she heard him mutter, 'My God!' Then he was turning back to her, kneeling by her chair, taking her hand as he used to do when she was a child.

'Cassie——' he began, and then, more gently, 'Cassie—I've been up to Lancashire. I've seen Ross Tyler. You know he's still alive, don't you?'

She nodded, and any doubts she may have felt about what Elaine had told her melted from her mind. It was obvious Neil had known nothing.

'I went to try and bring you back,' he continued, 'but you'd already left. I saw him—I saw Tyler. My God— I could hardly believe my eyes!' He was obviously finding it difficult to control his temper. 'He was as cool as a cucumber, too, almost as though he'd been expecting me!' He stopped, frowning. 'He said I was too late, that you'd already achieved what you'd been sent to do.

Cassie—what did he mean by that? What the hell was he talking about?'

Cassie stared at him mutely for a moment, her brain a mass of images, pictures from these last few days with Ross.

'I hardly know where to begin...' she explained wearily.

'Then begin at the beginning!' Neil said abruptly. 'Exactly when did all this start? When you went to see Bill Hodges—or before?'

'Neil!'

Natalie was emerging from the kitchen with a tray of coffee. She frowned at Neil before glancing pointedly at Cassie, and with an exclamation Neil stood up again, pacing restlessly across the rug before coming back to stand in front of Cassie again, staring down at her impotently.

'I'm sorry, darling, I don't mean to sound as if I'm giving you the third degree, but all this, it's—it's unbelievable! To think that all this time you've been mourning him—and damn near having a nervous breakdown in the process, I might add—and he's living up there, large as life, not giving a damn——'

'Neil!' Natalie exclaimed again, more worriedly this time, as Neil's voice began to rise yet again. She held out a mug of coffee. 'Here—sit down and drink this,' she suggested gently. 'You can see the state Cassie is in—let her explain in her own good time.'

Neil hesitated, the wisdom of Natalie's words obviously only just occurring to him, then with an abrupt word of thanks he took the coffee.

'Why don't you take your coat off as well?' Natalie suggested helpfully, her eyes on the heavy overcoat he was still wearing over his suit. Neil glanced down at himself in surprise, obviously having completely forgotten he was still wearing it, and, with a hint of impatience in the look he threw Natalie, he set his coffee down and shrugged off the coat, folding it carefully over the back of the armchair, before taking his coffee again and seating himself with a frustrated sigh.

Satisfied, Natalie placed a mug in front of Cassie then took her own from the tray, perching herself on the arm of Neil's chair and facing Cassie with a look of bewildered anxiety.

'How did you know I'd been to see Bill Hodges?' Cassie enquired carefully, addressing herself to Neil.

'Elaine told me,' he said, taking a gulp of his coffee. 'I only arrived back from New York yesterday afternoon. I'll admit I hoped you'd be there to meet me, Cassie,' he said, giving her a hard look, 'but when you weren't I headed straight back to the office. The phone was ringing as I walked through the door.' He took another gulp of his coffee. 'It was Elaine, wanting to know if you were with me. I could tell right away that something was wrong. When I said no, she very nearly had hysterics! It was very thoughtless of you, Cassie, to just go off like that,' he added, frowning at her. 'You could at least have told your mother——'

'So what did you do then?' Cassie interrupted tightly.

Neil finished his coffee and set his mug down, indicating to Natalie that he'd like another. 'Well,' he began, 'when I'd calmed her down a little she told me that all she knew was that you'd been to see Tyler's old editor, and then you'd apparently disappeared. So first thing this morning I went round to see the man for myself. He was surprised, I can tell you! Started babbling about libel actions and God knows what else, so I told him straight I was looking for you. He thrust a piece of paper at me with Tyler's address on it, and I drove straight up there.'

'I see.' Cassie spread her fingers in front of her, staring at them intently. 'So he didn't tell you it was Ross who wrote those articles about Brett's?'

'What?'

Natalie was kneeling by the coffee-table, in the act of pouring another cup of coffee for Neil. Her head jerked up in surprise and coffee went everywhere, but this was ignored as Neil leapt to his feet again, staring down at Cassie incredulously.

'You mean, *he's* the one who's been dragging Brett's through the mud these last few months?' he exclaimed angrily. 'He's the one who's brought us almost to the brink of financial ruin?'

Cassie nodded.

'But I don't understand!' Natalie exclaimed, looking even more bewildered than before. 'That doesn't sound like Ross at all! Why would he do something that he must have known would deliberately hurt you, Cassie?'

'Yes, what was his motive?' Neil interrupted. 'After all, you and he were practically——'

He stopped, frowning down at her, and Cassie supplied tonelessly, 'He believes I left him for dead after the accident.'

There was a stunned silence. Then, 'My God—the bastard!' Neil repeated violently. He swung away from Cassie to pace furiously across the rug. 'Now I'm beginning to understand!' he got out at last. 'It's all beginning to fall into place.' He swung back to face Cassie, his face suffusing with angry colour. 'He had some story about you having walked out on him. I didn't know what he was talking about. I told him, you thought he was dead—we *all* did!' Neil pushed his fingers through his hair, almost as though he couldn't keep them still. 'Well, he had some man there working for him—looked like a damned ex-boxer. He threatened to have me thrown out! Can you believe that? I told him not to bother, I was leaving anyway, but before I left I gave him some home-truths. I told him straight how it had been for you, what he'd put you through for the best part of two years, and all I can say now, Cassie, is thank God you didn't marry him——'

'Neil!' Natalie's cry of distress brought him to an abrupt halt. She got to her feet, facing him tremulously. 'You shouldn't say such things! You're only upsetting Cassie, and she's upset enough——'

'She's upset because she knows that pig has walked all over her!' Neil retorted bitingly. 'He's used her simply as a cover to filch information from Brett's. If you ask me, all this about her having walked out on him is just a con—because he never intended to marry her in the first place!'

Natalie's shocked face and Neil's furious features faded into blackness as Cassie realised with a sickening jolt that Neil had put into words her own innermost fears. Ever since Elaine had told her about Julia it had been gnawing away at her, and now she could ignore it no longer. The thought that she had been second-best, that Ross had never really loved her in the first place, was more than she could bear.

The lights along the Embankment flicked into life one by one, their brilliant haze adding a touch of warmth to the bitterly cold evening. But Cassie didn't even turn her head. She walked steadily on, collar turned up, head down, oblivious of hurrying passers-by.

This was the worst part of the day. Work was over and there was only the evening stretching emptily ahead, until it was time to get ready for bed and make a pretence of trying to get some sleep ready for another day. It was almost a relief to have to walk home, she thought. The garage had been remarkably prompt in taking her car in to have the paintwork done, and at least tonight she wouldn't have to face Natalie's anxious features over the dining-table. The strain of smiling, making conversation, putting a normal face over this misery inside her was almost unbearable at times. It was over a week since her return from Lancashire, but that didn't make the pain any easier to bear.

She turned at last into the mews. It was already dark, but she could make out the shadowy bulk of a car parked on their front, and wondered vaguely who it could be. Natalie was out, looking at possible premises for another boutique. She was supposed to have gone with her, but she had cried off at the last moment, suggesting Neil instead, and Natalie had jumped at the chance of having Neil's business acumen turned on their own small company. She had almost reached the car before she realised it was a Bentley, and, even as she halted uncertainly, the driver's door opened and Willis uncurled his long length from behind the wheel.

'Good evening, miss——' he began, but already another figure was detaching itself from the shadow of the houses, and suddenly she was face to face with Ross.

He was only using one stick, but something in the way he leant on it, and the way the streetlight fell across the harsh lines of his face, made her breath catch in her throat; but when he took a step towards her she hastily stepped back, glancing quickly to where Willis still stood by the car.

'Cassie——' he began, in a strange, almost breathless tone. 'I have to talk to you.'

She was silent, staring at him, and he continued abruptly, 'There are things I didn't understand before, but now we must talk——'

'There's nothing to talk about,' she got out, suddenly finding control of her voice again.

He seemed to hesitate, and then he muttered hoarsely, 'You must hear what I have to say, Cassie. Please.'

'I don't want to see you.'

There was a silence, and then he said abruptly, 'I realise that, and believe me, Cassie, if after this you still don't want to see me, then I'll understand. I'll go away and never bother you again.'

She was silent, and he continued hurriedly, 'You must hear me out, Cassie, just this once. It won't hurt too much to listen, will it?'

She stared at him, then nodded dumbly, and with another, final glance towards Willis she walked past him to put her key in the door.

He stood just behind her, she could feel him breathing, and then they were inside and she led the way into the sitting-room, flicking the lamps on and putting the width of the room between them before turning to face him mutely, her hands in her pockets.

He had closed the sitting-room door and was leaning back on it while his eyes flicked round the room. She noticed how pale he looked, surely paler than he had been a week ago? There were lines of weariness from nose to jaw. But he still managed to fill the room in a way that Neil had never been able to do.

His eyes came back to her.

'I've been to see Elaine,' he said at last. She was silent, staring at him, and he continued abruptly, 'Why didn't you tell me, Cassie? Why didn't you at least try to tell me that you...that she...'

'Would it have made any difference?' she asked, in a small, tight voice.

'Of course it would have made a difference!' he exploded violently. 'My God, Cassie, do you think I didn't *want* to believe you——?'

She stiffened and he stopped, checking himself, and ran a fraught hand through his hair. Then he said wearily, 'Do you mind if I sit down?'

'Yes, I do,' she snapped. 'Say what you have to say and get out!'

The sudden brutality in her voice caught him unawares, she could see that. He seemed to pale even further, and his eyes jerked back to her face, almost in disbelief.

'I know you have plenty of reasons to hate me, Cassie. I treated you very badly——'

'You're damn right!'

'But you must try to see it from my angle. I was terrified—terrified that if I welcomed you back with open arms you'd disappear again, like you did the last time——'

'You didn't love me.'

He stared at her incredulously. 'How can you say that?'

'If you'd loved me you would have known that I could never do anything so diabolical.'

'It was loving you that made it all so damned hard!' he contradicted fiercely. 'For God's sake, Cassie, I was in hospital—drugged up to the eyeballs! I was so ill and confused, I simply accepted what Elaine told me like a gullible fool. After all, she is your mother! It never occurred to me that she was—that she might be——' He drew a harsh breath. 'I'd investigated your grandfather—I'd investigated James—but I'd never even considered that Elaine could have a hand in it——'

'And Julia?'

There was a silence. He was breathing hard, as though he'd been running. 'Who told you about Julia?'

'Does it matter?'

'Elaine!' he gasped. 'My God—that woman has no scruples——'

'I asked you where you'd got that information and you wouldn't tell me!' she accused.

'Believe me, Cassie, there was nothing between us! Nothing happened——'

'Is that why you wouldn't tell me about it?' she asked, her voice heavy with accusation.

'You don't believe me, do you?' he got out.

'I think you'd better leave.'

That single taut sentence held him rigid; only a pulse beat erratically at his jaw. Her eyes came back up to his, and now she could see the torment in them, the desperate uncertainty that kept his shoulders hunched against the door.

For the first time, she thought, he's no longer in control of the situation; I am. And that thought gave her a feeling of grim satisfaction.

'I'll call Willis for you,' she said, in that same taut tone, and was already moving towards the door, but he put a hand out, and she stopped, not looking at him.

'No, Cassie, listen to me—please!' He took a breath. 'I came down here to try and talk to you, to try and explain to you why I did what I did. Surely you understand that? I thought if we could at least talk things through——'

'Like we did at The Breck?'

She thought he flinched. He had certainly paled. 'I was wrong, I admit that. I should never have treated you the way I did, but when you appeared on my doorstep that night, behaving as though—oh, God, you know how you behaved—it was as though the last two years had never happened. I wanted to wipe them away, Cassie, you'll never know how much—but I couldn't! It had been eating away at me for eighteen months and I was obsessed with what I thought you'd done to me—to us! That's why I had to come and see you now, to try and prevent it happening again——' He paused, swallowing hard. 'I thought if we could at least begin to talk things through——'

'I'm through talking.'

He was silent, staring at her. 'You don't mean that.'

'You said yourself, there are too many other things between us.'

'There's nothing that can't be overcome——'

'Even without trust?' The pleasure it gave her to fling his words back at him was a physical pain.

'I know how you must feel—about Julia,' he got out. 'But believe me, Cassie, if you'll at least give me a chance to explain, then perhaps in time you'll understand——'

'No.'

There was nothing but the sound of his breathing and the ticking of the clock on the mantelpiece, and then he burst out desperately, 'For God's sake, Cassie, we were happy once!'

'Happy?' she echoed hollowly. 'That was two years ago, Ross, and the way I feel now, it might as well be an eternity.'

'Then at least give me time——'

'I don't want to see you,' she repeated tonelessly. 'I don't know how you got my address, I suppose it was from my mother, but I'd be obliged if you didn't come here again. As you say, perhaps in time I'll learn to forgive and forget, but at the moment I don't want to see you, Ross. I don't want to speak to you, I don't want to have any contact with you whatsoever. Do you understand?'

His face was grey now, held together by lines of pain. 'If that is what you really want,' he said at last, and his voice was cracked and strained.

'It is.'

She could see him hesitating, considering a last, desperate appeal.

'You're hurting me, Cassie, you know that. You're trying to pay me back for what I've done to you. You're succeeding too, but believe me, I've been down that road; you'll only end up destroying yourself——'

'Get out!' she flung at him, shaking suddenly.

He stared at her for a full minute, then slowly he straightened away from the door and his fingers tautened whitely round the top of his stick.

The door closed behind him.

She listened for the sound of the front door closing, and the purr of the Bentley's engine, and when all was quiet again she sank to the rug and collapsed into silent, searing sobs.

CHAPTER SEVEN

THE LEASE for the new shop premises was signed and sealed, and preparations for the new boutique were well in hand. Natalie was already fretting over lighting and shop fitters and colour schemes, and frantic with worry that her designs for next season were behind schedule; but the designs would be on time, Cassie knew. Natalie had always been the same, even at school: completely lacking in any kind of self-confidence while at the same time producing brilliant designs for the sets for the school play; and her designs *were* brilliant, even Neil had to admit that. In fact Neil seemed to be showing an interest in the boutique that Cassie would have found unbelievable two months ago, and she began to wonder if James and, through him, Elaine, had anything to do with this growing involvement in their business affairs.

She hadn't seen her mother since that night she'd returned from Lancashire, but, if any of the family thought it strange, nothing had been said openly about it. Only Neil had commented on the fact that she wasn't going home for Christmas. The only other person she'd seen was James, when she'd been to visit her grandfather in hospital, and when he mentioned it she had told him simply that she was spending Christmas with Natalie and her family, and he had accepted it without question. Apparently Julia, too, would be away. She and Roddy were going on holiday for a couple of weeks. They need the break, James had said, in his usual bluff fashion, but her grandfather had been more scathing.

'They're going to try and save their marriage!' he'd declared bluntly. 'I gave them an ultimatum. Divorce these days is too expensive, and at the moment we can't afford the publicity!'

Her grandfather was back on form. He at least would be home for Christmas, and, though he would have a nurse with him, her parents would have their hands full coping with his demands without the added complications of her and Julia.

Only Neil didn't seem to have made any plans for Christmas, and Cassie realised guiltily that this was partly her fault; but there was nothing she could do about it. She thought he would have realised by now, but he seemed intent on playing some silent, waiting game of his own. He had been fussing over her like a mother hen these last few weeks, and, though she could see now where it was all leading up to, still she had no wish to hurt him. She would try and let him down gently, if that were at all possible.

He was insisting on taking her out at Christmas for a 'special celebration', as he called it. Just the two of them. He had already booked a show and a meal at a fashionably exclusive restaurant. It was something she could have done without, but she had done what was expected of her and accepted graciously, and rather than let him down she had dressed in her finery, determined to try and enter into the spirit of Christmas on this occasion at least, for Neil's sake, if not for her own. But from the beginning the evening did not go as planned. Neil's meticulous arrangements had not taken into account the Christmas lights, or the Christmas traffic, and as their taxi crawled to a halt yet again he leant forward, peering past the dark bulk of the driver and muttering in barely suppressed annoyance, 'We shouldn't have come this way—damn! I knew it would be like this. We'll never make dinner in time now!'

With a barely audible sigh Cassie turned, and there was the glint of diamonds from the depths of her hooded fur jacket. 'I'm not really hungry,' she murmured placatingly, and put her hand out to cover his, stilling the insistent tapping of his fingers on his knee. 'Why don't we get out and walk for a while?'

Neil sat back with a hiss of resigned frustration. 'Those shoes of yours weren't made for walking,' he pointed out testily. 'And besides, I'd booked the table specially. We only got in because I'm well in with Carlo.'

'I'm sorry,' she said gently. 'It's my fault. If I hadn't wanted to see the lights . . .'

He sighed heavily, staring down at her hand covering his. 'No,' he said. 'It's my fault, Cassie. I'm being a boor, and I'm sorry. I'd planned this evening as something special, and it's not going at all as I'd hoped——'

'But it has been special,' she interrupted, trying to inject as much enthusiasm as she could into her voice. 'It's ages since we've been out together like this, and I enjoyed the show enormously——'

'The show was only part of it,' he interrupted, a hint of petulance in his voice now. 'I wanted the whole evening to be special, something we could both remember.' He stopped, hesitating, and then began in a deeper tone, 'Cassie——'

'Neil——' she began hurriedly, and tried to pull her hand away, but where a few seconds ago her fingers had been resting lightly on his, now, suddenly, her hand was enclosed in both of his. 'Neil, I'm not blind to what you've been trying to do for me these last few weeks,' she continued gently. 'I don't know what I'd have done without your support. You've been a good friend, and I'm grateful, you know that——'

'I'm trying to show you how much you mean to me, Cassie,' he interrupted tautly.

'Neil, you don't have to prove anything——'

'But I do!' he contradicted earnestly. 'I'm trying to prove to you that I—that I——'

He stopped, staring at her, and then with a harsh sigh he collapsed back against the seat again. He passed a hand across his eyes, as though in weariness, and then he said in a completely altered tone, 'What's the point? You don't hear me, do you, Cassie? I might just as well be beating my head against a brick wall!'

She didn't pretend to misunderstand him. 'I'm sorry, Neil,' she said quietly.

'You still love him, don't you?'

Cassie turned back to the window, staring bleakly out at the lines of glistening traffic, the brilliant dancing lights, and the crowds of pedestrians silhouetted against the enticing glare of the shops.

'Yes,' she whispered. 'I do.' It was the first time she'd admitted it, even to herself.

'Then why don't you stop torturing yourself and go back to him?'

'I can't,' she said, a catch in her voice that made him grip her hand even tighter. 'I can't, Neil! There are too many things between us, and besides, you said yourself——'

'I said a lot of things, Cassie,' he interrupted harshly. 'A lot of things that should never have been said. That night I came back from Lancashire I was angry. Angry with Tyler, angry with myself—and yes, even angry with you!' She turned back to him and he continued wryly, 'When you ran away to France after that silly row we had, it made me stop and think. I realised then that you needed more time. And then, suddenly, Tyler was back on the scene and time was one thing I didn't have. As soon as I saw your face that night, I knew I was fighting a losing battle. You looked—oh, God knows how you looked, but I knew he could never have hurt you that much if you hadn't still cared for him, even just a little.'

'I thought I hated him,' she said simply, remembering that final, brutal meeting with Ross. 'I *tried* to hate him. Even now I'm only just beginning to come to terms with how I feel.' She sighed. 'It would have been so much simpler if it had been you, Neil. I wish it *had* been you. I'm sorry.'

'So am I.' He took her hand again, patting it gently. 'So am I, Cassie. But at least we can still be friends, can't we?'

She nodded, smiling in spite of herself. 'Yes, Neil. We can still be friends.'

'Then, as a friend, tell me why you can't go back and sort things out with Tyler.'

He was watching her, waiting, frowning thoughtfully, and she turned away, staring out of the window again. 'I just can't, Neil.'

'But surely, if you explain the facts——'

'I spent four days trying to explain the facts!' she interrupted bitterly, unable to hide her pain any longer. 'Or at least, what I *thought* were the facts! But you were right that night, Neil, when you said he'd never really loved me in the first place. It was what I'd half feared myself, only I'd been too much of a coward to admit it! He was simply using me—using me for information so that he could write those articles—and they were the principle cause of my grandfather's heart attack!'

Her voice was rising almost to the point of hysteria as it all came pouring out, all the misery and anger and bitterness she had tried so hard to keep in check. With a stifled sob she collapsed against the seat, shaking with silent tears, and after a moment Neil's arms came round her and she was gathered to him in a comforting embrace.

'Cassie!' he scolded soothingly. 'Cassie, you've kept it all bottled up inside yourself for so long, I'm surprised it hasn't driven you insane! It's time you talked about it. Perhaps if we talk it through, clearly and rationally, we can come up with some answers——'

'I can't, Neil,' she hiccuped. 'I can't talk about it—not yet!'

'Yes, you can,' he chided gently. 'And besides, you owe it to me, Cassie. You owe me that, at least.'

Her sobs were quietening. With a last, shuddering sigh she pulled away from him, staring up at him with tear-stained eyes, and he continued grimly, 'I've been giving it a lot of thought since I came back from Lancashire, Cassie, and though I've no idea how or why, it's clear to me now that he really did believe you'd walked out on him.'

His look was speculative, but she was silent, searching for her handkerchief. She hadn't told anyone of Elaine's part in all this. She couldn't. And it would probably all come out soon enough anyway. She was sure that Ross would lose no time in vindicating his uncle, and for the last couple of weeks she had been dreading seeing the morning newspapers, expecting to see the whole sordid story splashed across the headlines, with a picture of Elaine being led away in handcuffs, or something equally drastic. And besides, Neil worked with James. It might make things awkward for him if he knew.

She closed her eyes as fresh misery engulfed her. *Her own mother!* Sometimes she thought it was that that hurt most of all . . .

'Tyler must have been as mad as hell-fire,' Neil continued, handing her his own immaculate white handkerchief. 'I'm damn sure he wrote those articles simply to get back at you, but as for your grandfather's heart attack . . .' He moved his shoulders, settling himself back in his seat again as the taxi once more began to move forward. 'There's no way he could have foreseen that. It was pure coincidence.'

'You can't be sure of that,' Cassie mumbled from the depths of the handkerchief. 'He hates us, Neil. He hates us *all*——'

'I'm as sure of that as I am of anything,' Neil responded firmly. 'There's something you should know, Cassie, something you should have known ages ago but your grandfather wanted it kept quiet. He was worried about how it would affect Brett's on the stock market if it ever got out, and he insisted none of the family should know. But there seems no point now in keeping quiet——'

'Keeping quiet about what?' Cassie asked, dabbing carefully at what was left of her make-up. 'What are you talking about, Neil?'

'Your grandfather has a heart condition,' Neil said gently. 'He's known about it for three or four years.'

Cassie was suddenly still, staring at him.

'I only found out myself just after his heart attack,' Neil continued. 'James told me; apparently he was the only other person who knew—apart from your grandfather's doctor, of course. So you see, your grandfather could have collapsed at any time. It was pure coincidence it happened when it did. Under the circumstances, your grandfather has got off very lightly.'

Cassie had turned back to the window again, staring silently out as the taxi sped them away from the brilliant haze that was Regent Street.

'Well? Doesn't that make you feel a little better?' Neil asked, when she didn't speak. 'At least you know now that, whatever else Tyler may have done, he had nothing to do with your grandfather's illness.'

'There are—other things, Neil,' she got out in a low, harsh voice.

'Other things?' Neil asked, leaning forward. 'What other things, Cassie? Tell me.'

She hesitated, biting her lip, then she said tautly, 'Other women.'

He was staring at her in puzzlement, but her eyes were fixed on her fingers now, spread out straight and taut against her silk-clad knees.

'When I went to see him that weekend,' she began carefully, 'he had a woman staying with him. *A woman.*' She swallowed painfully. 'I couldn't believe it at first. I'd been eating my heart out for months, and he'd already turned to someone else for consolation!'

Neil eyed the pale oval of her taut features. 'Well, I don't know anything about a woman, Cassie, but that day I saw him he was in a hell of a state over your leaving——'

Cassie looked up. 'A hell of a state?' she echoed sharply. 'What do you mean by that? You told me he threatened to have you thrown out! You said he——'

'I know what I said!' Neil interrupted impatiently. 'You don't have to remind me, Cassie. I haven't been able to get it out of my mind ever since, thinking that—well, perhaps I gave you the wrong impression——'

'The wrong impression?' she echoed, staring at him. 'What do you mean?'

He shifted restlessly, his eyes sliding away from hers. 'I've already admitted I was angry that night, Cassie. I said a lot of things that should never have been said. Oh—it's true he threatened to have me thrown out. It's true too that we argued, but not in the way you think. He was like a wild man, Cassie, but it was the wildness of despair. He was like a tiger caught in a trap of his own making. He thought he'd lost you, and I can see now what that was doing to him.'

'That still doesn't excuse what he's done,' she said in a small, tight voice.

'No, but it might help you to see things in perspective.' His eyes came back to hers. 'You can't go on as you are, Cassie. You're destroying yourself, and sooner or later you're going to have to come to some sort of decision. Either you forget him completely and get on with the rest of your life—or you go back and try and sort out your differences.'

'You're trying to run my life for me, Neil,' she said in that same tight voice.

'No, Cassie, I'm merely offering you advice. As a friend.'

She stared at him for a moment, stiff and upright in her corner of the taxi, and then slowly she expelled her breath on a long sigh and ran her fingers through her hair in a futile movement of despair.

'Perhaps you're right,' she admitted at long last, and deep down she had to acknowledge the truth of what he said. She couldn't go on like this, being torn to pieces inside. She had never expected Ross to follow her to London the way he had, and in her pain and misery she had been guilty of the very same thing she had accused him of. She had thought she hated him, and she had wanted to hurt him the way he had hurt her. But now that first ferment of bitter, vengeful anger had subsided and she felt empty, aimless in a fog of cold misery. Trust Neil to cut straight to the heart of the matter. His cool logic had cut through all her emotional shilly-shallying. He had always been able to stand back from a problem, to view it objectively from both sides, no matter what his personal involvement. It was that that made him such a good businessman, she supposed, but she could not be so detached.

'I *can't* forget, Neil,' she said simply. 'That's what makes it so hard. But as for the other...' She turned to stare bleakly out of the window again. 'Well—I'll have to think about it, Neil. I'll have to think about it.'

But she didn't. She shut Neil's words away in the back of her mind, and even though she was aware of them niggling away at the edges of her consciousness she refused to take them out and consider them further. She couldn't. The pain was still too intense, and even though she was vaguely aware that her perspectives were beginning to alter, that the pain inside her was shifting to a different level, still she knew it was too soon. And besides, once Christmas was over she and Natalie were in a flat spin to get the new boutique ready for a grand opening, and she hardly had time to think, let alone to brood over her own unhappiness.

The New Year opened on a frenzy of activity, but as the weeks began to flash past with increasing speed she began to realise that she couldn't go on avoiding her mother for ever. They had a preliminary rehearsal for the fashion show to publicise the opening, and already Neil was dropping subtle hints about inviting her parents.

'I don't know why you're so against it,' he said, when he realised his subtlety was having no effect. 'To be fair, James has always been interested in how well the boutique is doing, and he has turned a blind eye to the fact that over these last few weeks I've been as much involved with your business affairs as I have with Brett's. And even your mother can see the potential now.'

I'll bet she can! Cassie thought bitterly, and then raised her shoulders in a weary shrug. What was the point in bitterness now? She'd never had any illusions about where her mother's priorities lay, had she? And what was done was done. There was no way she could go back and alter the past. Besides, she was even beginning to feel a little sorry for Elaine. Apparently she had been ill since Christmas. Stress-induced, the doctor had said, according to Neil. And Cassie had no illusions as to exactly where that stress was coming from. These days she couldn't wait for the morning papers to arrive, scanning even the society columns in an attempt to discover why they had still heard nothing from Ross, or his solicitors, and the strain must be telling on Elaine. Everything was running smoothly at Brett's, otherwise Neil would have mentioned it, and she began to wonder if this was some new game Ross was playing. Was his continued silence designed to grind them all down, so that eventually Elaine was so guilt-ridden she voluntarily bared her soul to the world?

'Your mother has been asking about you a lot just lately,' Neil persisted, and so Cassie found herself reluctantly acquiescing.

'I suppose you're right,' she sighed. Elaine was her mother, after all. 'Perhaps you think I should invite Grandfather Brett as well?' she added, with some sarcasm, but Neil merely grinned.

'There's no need. He's already invited himself.'

Perhaps it was only natural that Neil would keep the family up to date on what was happening at the boutique; after all, he was still a regular visitor to James's house. But it was a complete surprise to everyone during the final week of preparations when her grandfather arrived unexpectedly in his chauffeured limousine.

He sat in his wheelchair, viewing the models' perambulations through shrewdly narrowed eyes, and afterwards Cassie accused him fraughtly of giving everyone the jitters.

'You know absolutely nothing about the fashion industry!' she told him, but he merely shrugged his massive shoulders.

'Fashion industry or not, it's all business.'

'Well—what do you think?' she asked. She was pouring boiling water into two cups of instant coffee. It was all she seemed to have time for these days.

'It looks good,' he said. 'But then I knew it would if Neil was involved.'

'Oh, thanks!' she responded, with some sarcasm, and handed him his coffee.

'What I really want to know,' he continued, giving her a quick look, 'is what you're going to do when all this is over.'

She stirred her coffee. 'Well, in another few months there'll probably be another boutique to open, and another, and another——'

'Don't be flippant with me, young lady!' he told her, frowning. 'You know very well what I mean! It's about time you settled down——'

Her eyes jerked to his face, her own smile completely gone now. 'I'm not Julia, Grandfather. And I'm not going to marry Neil——'

His eyebrows rose. 'Who said anything about Neil?'

A shock ran through her as she met his look, and suddenly it was an effort to keep the cup steady in her hands. She set it down.

'I'm not quite the old fool your mother takes me for,' he continued shrewdly. 'You've been like a wet rag since before Christmas, and don't think I haven't noticed too that you haven't been to see me since I've been at your parents' house. It's Elaine, isn't it?'

She nodded dumbly.

'I won't embarrass you, Cassie, but I know it's something to do with that journalist you were going to marry a couple of years ago—Tyler. She put a stop to it, didn't she?' Cassie couldn't speak, and he continued grimly, 'It was he who wrote those articles about Brett's last year.'

Cassie swallowed painfully. 'I suppose Neil told you.'

'No, he didn't. Let's just say, I made enquiries. I didn't get where I am today by sitting on my backside, Cassandra, and you'd do well to remember that. Despite what everyone thinks, I've had to fight damned hard, and you'd do well to remember that, too.' He paused. 'As to where Tyler got his information——'

Cassie's eyes widened as his narrowed thoughtfully, and then he was continuing abruptly, 'However, that doesn't matter now—and besides, it's already been dealt with. What does matter is that the inquiry into Brett's affairs found nothing to be concerned about. In fact, Brett's came out of it with glowing colours, and in some respects business has been much brisker since. What concerns me now, however, is the family itself—and the hold Tyler has over us.'

Cassie groped for a chair and sank into it, her face white and set.

'You knew,' she whispered accusingly. 'You've known all along!'

He hesitated. 'I was suspicious, yes.'

'Then why didn't you do something—anything?'

For the first time, Alexander Brett looked away from her accusing glare. 'There was nothing I could do.'

'Nicholas Daleford was your friend——' she began incredulously.

'And James is my son!' he underlined grimly. 'Blood is thicker than water, Cassandra!'

With an exclamation he raised a hand to his forehead, rubbing it impatiently. 'You must understand, my dear. James was already in his forties, and married to Brett's, as I was. I'd given up all hope of grandchildren to inherit the firm. Then he went up to Manchester on a routine visit, and within weeks he was talking of marriage. How could I tell him I suspected the only woman he'd ever cared for of industrial espionage? Anyhow, the contract was already well under way. It could have meant the end of Brett's, as well as Daleford's.'

'So you simply cut Nicholas Daleford out of your life!'

He moved his shoulders. 'He was in Manchester—I was in London. And if what I suspected about my son's new wife was true——' He paused. 'Nicholas Daleford was one of the most honest, upright men I've ever known. He was open-hearted, too, perhaps that's why he took the boy in as he did, but it meant that he never suspected his own people. Perhaps if he'd paid as much attention to what was happening at the firm as he did to the boy, then things might have turned out differently. As it is—by the time I knew what was happening, it was too late.'

'And later, when Ross turned up at Brett's?' Cassie demanded tautly.

Her grandfather shrugged again. 'I decided to let events run their course. I knew Elaine knew who he was. It was simply a question of waiting to see what she would do.'

'You gambled on her getting rid of him!' Cassie accused hoarsely. 'My God—and she accused Ross of manipulating people——'

'My main concern has always been the family!' Alexander Brett contradicted determinedly. 'No matter what our personal differences, Cassandra, we've always presented a united front to the world. We're Bretts, and we stick together.'

'So you let my mother ruin *my* life for the sake of the family?'

'Elaine has always been strong-willed and ruthlessly ambitious—she wouldn't be where she is today if she weren't.'

'You expect me to *forgive* her for what she's done?'

'I don't *expect* anything!' he bit out. 'But she's cracking up, Cassandra. She's on the edge of a nervous breakdown. Tyler knows, doesn't he?'

She was silent, and he continued relentlessly, 'Why hasn't he done something about it? What is he waiting for, Cassandra?'

Cassie ran her fingers through her hair in a quick, tense movement, and then suddenly her shoulders sagged. 'I don't know,' she admitted tautly. 'But whatever it is, it has nothing to do with me.'

'Are you sure?'

She swung round, staring at him, the shadows under her eyes indicative of the strain she was under; but somehow they only seemed to emphasise the vulnerability in the depths of her green eyes, and the set lines of her pale face.

His voice softened. 'Whatever else she may be, Elaine is still your mother, Cassandra. You're as aware of that as anyone. So is Tyler. He did what he felt he had to do, and I don't hold that against him, so why should you?' He paused, eyeing her set features, the rigid line of her jaw, and then he continued gently, 'When you get to my age, my girl, you'll begin to realise that life is too short for fretting about what might have been. If you want something, then you have to reach out and grab it with both hands, because if you miss your chance, you rarely get another.'

'Well, here's to success!' Mandy grinned, and her glass clinked loudly against Cassie's. It was the party to celebrate the opening of the boutique, and the fashion show that had preceded it had been a brilliant success, even Cassie had to admit that. Mandy was over from Paris with David, her husband, and even she seemed a little overawed. 'How does it *feel* to be a success?'

'Fine.' Cassie sipped her champagne and let her eyes move slowly around the glittering, crowded room. Most of the people she didn't know personally she knew by name or reputation. The publicity for the show had been phenomenal.

'You could sound a little more pleased about it,' Mandy retorted.

'Neil arranged most of the invitations,' Cassie stated flatly, and looked across to where Neil stood with Natalie, his head bent attentively to a potential customer.

'You arranged everything else,' Mandy pointed out. 'And even though Natalie's clothes are out of this world, the pair of you couldn't have chosen a better way of showing them off. Those settings were superb. I told you it would all work out!'

Cassie smiled. 'Yes, you did.' Her holiday in Paris seemed like years ago now. Was it only six months since she had been dithering about whether or not to go into partnership with Natalie, or take the final step and marry Neil?

'Well, how does it feel?'

Cassie's eyes were still on the crowded room, the smiling faces, the upraised glasses. 'After all the work we've put in these last weeks, arranging contracts, shop fitters, decorators, models—and all the rest of it, I had some vague idea that today it would all be over. Instead, I've realised suddenly that it's only just beginning.'

It had hit her like a bolt from the blue this afternoon that the independence, the success she had always wanted was finally hers, and she knew she should feel elated. But when she looked round the room, felt the electricity in the air, she knew she didn't quite share that same excitement. She couldn't quite feel that upsurge of joy, that heady aura of success. Something was missing, and she wasn't sure what.

She looked across at Natalie again. Her cheeks were flushed, her eyes shining. Who would have believed that for the last week she had been white-faced, almost physically sick with nerves, surviving almost entirely on tea and coffee and that intense nervous energy she always seemed to produce at times of stress? But now, even her shyness seemed to have deserted her. She was smiling at something Neil had said, blushing even more as his arm came to rest across her shoulders in an unconsciously possessive gesture that Cassie found vaguely familiar.

'It looks as though there's going to be another partner in the business before very long,' Mandy murmured. She, too, was watching Neil and Natalie.

'I'd say it was a distinct possibility.'

'Don't you mind?' Mandy's look was sharply probing. 'After all, you and he were almost——'

'Just good friends,' Cassie declared lightly, and smiled. 'I was thinking only the other day how well they get on together. Natalie always did need someone to protect her from the harsh realities of life, and Neil fits the bill perfectly.'

Someone waved from the other side of the room, and they both smiled and waved back. It was David, gesturing desperately towards the buffet table. Mandy nodded and looked at Cassie, but Cassie shook her head, and with a murmured apology Mandy left her to make her way across to her husband.

Left alone, Cassie sipped her champagne, her eyes once again wandering round the room. She noticed the solid figure of her grandfather in his wheelchair, and, standing behind him, James and Elaine. Her meeting with her mother earlier had been restrained, to say the least, but inwardly she had been shocked at Elaine's haggard look. Her grandfather had only touched the tip of the iceberg when he had said she was cracking up, and though Cassie had only had time for a brief, cool smile before being whisked away to meet other, more important guests, her mother's pale features seemed to have been hanging over her all afternoon.

She stared into her champagne, frowning heavily, and then in an abrupt movement she raised the glass to her lips and drained it, before turning to set it down, but as she did so another figure caught her eye, and she stiffened, her fingers automatically tightening round the stem of the glass. Her eyes focused on dark, velvety curls and eyes that somehow matched, and she went rigid with shock. She hadn't been mistaken; Elise was moving purposefully towards her from the other side of the room, and before she could even move the other woman was upon her, a smile on her face, her hand outstretched.

'Cassie—I knew I wasn't mistaken! How nice to see you again.'

The voice hadn't changed, and neither had the smile. Cassie's cold fingers fluttered jerkily out towards Elise's smooth, warm ones and withdrew again almost immediately.

'I knew I wasn't mistaken!' Elise repeated silkily. 'I saw your picture in the newspapers and I recognised you immediately. What a sly thing you are!' The smile was amused, but the eyes were as cold as ever. 'You told me you worked in a boutique, and naturally I assumed...'

She didn't finish, allowing her words to hang in the air as her delicate eyebrows rose meaningfully.

Cassie managed a smile. After the initial shock she was recovering quickly, one thought uppermost in her mind.

'Are—are you alone?'

The question sounded almost casual, but Elise's momentary hesitation, her narrowed look, seemed to Cassie to bring the whole room to a standstill.

'No, I'm with my fiancé.'

The shock now was absolute. Cassie couldn't speak. Her eyes were fixed on Elise's immaculate features, while her mind was running frantically round the room, mentally inspecting all the faces that had passed before her in the last hour.

Her shock had obviously communicated itself to Elise. 'Didn't you know?' she murmured silkily. 'Surely you saw the announcement in *The Times*?'

'I've—I've been rather busy——'

Elise smiled. 'Oh, yes, of course. It must have been quite something, putting all this together.' Her eyes flicked round the room. 'I must say, my dear, I couldn't have done better myself. But then, being who you are, money wouldn't be a problem, would it?' Her eyes came back to Cassie. 'Would you like to meet him—my fiancé, that is?'

Cassie was struggling to regain her earlier composure. 'Well—I don't think——'

But Elise had already threaded her arm through Cassie's and was leading her forward, and Cassie's eyes darted frantically round the room while Elise murmured in her ear, 'It's all very romantic really—he doesn't normally let me out of his sight, you know. He's devoted to me—sweet, isn't it?'

A sea of faces swam in front of Cassie, while inside she was shaking with panic. Ross wasn't here—*he couldn't be!* Surely she would have seen him? But then, Neil had sent out all the invitations—Neil! Surely he would have said something? Or Natalie? Or Mandy——?

'Here he is!' The note of triumph in Elise's voice brought Cassie's head round with a jerk. The sea of faces resolved themselves into one. But there were no piercing grey eyes, no thick dark hair. Merely round, almost bland features hidden behind glasses and a rather large bow-tie.

'Cassandra Beresford—this is Donald—Donald Cochrane. He's in design too, you know,' Elise smiled. 'In the States.'

Cassie felt dazed, almost weak with relief. 'An American?' Her hand came out automatically and was clasped in a huge, warm paw.

'Only half-American, Miss Beresford,' he grinned. 'My grandpa was a Scot. I'm over here to view my inheritance—that's how I met Elise. My grandpa left me a castle in Scotland, y'know.' He paused, grinning even more at this piece of information. 'It's going to take some doing up—it'll keep me and Elise busy for quite a while!'

'Does that mean you've—finished—at The Breck?' Cassie asked, looking at Elise, and Elise raised slim shoulders in a brief shrug.

'My dear—I never really *started* at The Breck, did I? After your arrival that weekend, Ross lost all interest in interior design. That was why I left—surely you realised that? And anyway,' she continued smoothly, 'The Breck

was so isolated. Donald's castle has *much* more potential.' She turned to bestow a brilliant smile on her
fiancé, and Cassie suddenly felt like hugging her.

'I'm very pleased for you,' she said, smiling.

'We've come down to London to make arrangements
for the wedding,' Elise purred, and Donald Cochrane's
grin was transferred from Cassie to Elise and back again.

'Sure thing. Elise's huntin' for her trousseau, y'know.
She wanted to see your collection, Miss Beresford, and
I must say—I'm impressed!'

'I'm glad you like it.' Cassie was still smiling. It seemed
a natural thing to do. She was under no illusions as to
why Elise was really here—no doubt after seeing her
photograph in the newspapers Elise had determined to
come here today and see for herself what it was all about.
But that didn't seem to matter now. All that did matter
was that suddenly Cassie felt like smiling again.

She beckoned a passing waiter, and when he had ex-
changed their empty glasses for full ones she began
matter-of-factly, 'I think this calls for a toast, don't you?
And as this is obviously such a special occasion for you
both, I think we can manage a little discount on anything you may decide to buy from our boutiques. Shall
we say—ten percent?'

A smug, satisfied smile had crept across Elise's face.
'That's very thoughtful of you, Cassie,' she murmured
silkily.

'Sure is,' Donald Cochrane interposed. 'Very
thoughtful, indeed! And if we can ever put any business
your way in the future, Miss Beresford, we sure will. In
fact, if there's ever anything else we can do——'

But Cassie was already raising her glass. 'Here's to a castle in Scotland,' she murmured, smiling. And when they had all drunk, she left Elise to her self-satisfied smile and her fiancé to his overflowing appreciation, and went off to find Natalie and Neil.

CHAPTER EIGHT

THE HILLS no longer looked dark and forbidding, but more as she remembered them from those long-ago days with her father: green and beginning to smile again in the thin, watery sunshine of an April evening. Even the road seemed different: shorter, and not quite as twisting. But perhaps, she thought, that was because this time she knew where she was going.

She passed a couple of houses, and then her nerves leapt as she recognised the garage she had driven to that Monday morning with Willis. George, the mechanic, was on the forecourt serving petrol, and he looked up as she sped past, but her face was averted. Her eyes had leapt away from him almost as soon as she recognised his overall-clad figure. But then, he wouldn't have recognised her anyway, she thought, with a wry twist of her lips.

She was watching the road now, looking for signs. A familiar sweep of field; the curve of a hill. And all the while the car was slowing, until her foot was barely touching the accelerator and she was travelling at a less-than-steady twenty miles an hour.

She came to the stone gateposts and stopped, staring at them rigidly, for a full five minutes. She had come almost to his doorstep, and suddenly she was a mass of nerves.

And she wasn't even sure why she had come. Was it for Elaine—or simply for herself? All she knew was that these last few days she had been doing an awful lot of thinking: thinking about the past, thinking about the future, but mainly, thinking about Ross.

Seeing Elise again seemed to have finally released something inside her. The numbing coldness that had held her in thrall for what seemed like an eternity was finally giving way to something else—hope, perhaps? Whatever it was, that black cloud of depression had finally lifted and she had begun to live again, to come to terms with the past. But before she could consider the future she knew she had to see Ross again, to make this journey just one more time.

The thought crossed her mind that perhaps he would refuse to see her, would reject her as he had done once before—but she pushed that thought away almost as soon as it entered her head. No, after that last time in London...but then that last time it had been her turn to be cruel. Perhaps now she had no right to hope. Perhaps since then he had changed his mind, finally decided to put her out of his life...

Well, she was too close to turn back now, and after all the heartsearching of these last months she *couldn't* turn back.

She crunched the car into gear again and continued on up the lane, in at the new gates, and along the sweep of gravel.

And there was the house.

She parked at the front and reached for her bag. The familiarity of it all was vaguely reassuring, but she wasn't going to appear over-confident by driving into the yard.

She climbed out of the car and looked around.

The hills, the trees, the stretch of lawn, were just as she remembered them; only the creeper over the front of the house was different. The breathtaking red of autumn had given way to bare, spidery tentacles that clung blindly to the old stone, giving the front of the house a faintly dilapidated air that hadn't been noticeable before. And the new buds of spring were only just beginning to show.

She climbed the steps, knocked at the door, and waited. There was no reply, so she knocked again, louder this time, and waited again. But still no one came, and she stared helplessly at the blank face of the door. Surely she hadn't come all this way only to find there was no one in? Where were Dora and Willis?

It was beginning to get dark now; dusk was falling rapidly, and she pulled the collar of her coat up as a sudden chill breeze sent the last year's leaves swirling and dancing across the gravel. Without further hesitation she descended the steps again and began to walk briskly round to the back of the house, looking in windows on the way. But there were no lights, no signs of life at all, and that first stab of disappointment began to deepen into something more apprehensive.

The kitchen door was closed, but when she tried the handle it opened, and she stepped inside. The kitchen, too, was deserted, but at least it was warm, and she went across to the Aga and held her cold hands out to its heat. At least someone was in residence, she thought, eyeing the kitchen table with the half-eaten remains of a meal still spread over it. There were dirty dishes in the sink, too, and empty cans and other assorted items spread over the units. The kitchen looked a mess. She went along the passage into the hall and gave a tentative shout, but her own voice echoed emptily back at her, and after a moment she retreated back to the kitchen and stood with her bag clasped in front of her, looking round at the debris in perplexed uncertainty.

Perhaps she should go back to the car? she thought. But even as she took a step towards the door there was the sound of footsteps on the cobbled yard, and the next moment Ross himself appeared, stick in hand, his frame, in its heavy waterproof, almost filling the doorway, and mud-splattered wellingtons on his feet.

He stared at her, and surprise—and shock—held her rigid.

God, he looks terrible, she thought. He looked as though he hadn't shaved for a week, but that hardly mattered. What did matter were the deeply etched lines of his face, the red-rimmed, hooded eyes, and the weary pallor of his thin features. And how thin he was. Even in the heavy waterproof she could see he'd lost weight. It was open down the front, revealing an Aran wool jumper and worn cords that seemed to hang off him. Her eyes came back up to his.

He moved then, advancing into the kitchen and closing the door behind him, before turning back to face her. He was still watching her, his eyes dark and intent, but there was no surprise in his face.

'I saw the car at the front,' he stated flatly, as though in answer to her unspoken question. And then, 'Why have you come, Cassie?'

The question seemed to hang in the air between them, and it was a moment before she could bring herself to speak.

'I—I came to see you,' she said simply.

His mouth twisted. 'I would have thought that was obvious. What I want to know is—why?'

He seemed almost—hostile, and her stomach plunged with misery. His features were taut and unyielding, but then, what had she expected—that he would welcome her with open arms? She glanced helplessly round the kitchen.

'Ross—why are you alone here?' she got out at last, answering his question with one of her own. 'And what have you been doing to yourself? You look absolutely——'

'I've been out for a walk,' he interrupted flatly.

Her eyes flicked over the wellingtons. 'But I didn't see you when I drove up the road——?'

'That's because I didn't walk up the road,' he interrupted again, and her eyes jerked back to his face.

'Surely you haven't been out on the hill?'

'Why not?'

She stared at him, pictures in her mind of the rough moorland, with him stumbling—perhaps falling—with no help at hand——

'But it's freezing up there!' she burst out. 'And your legs——'

'My legs are fine!' he snapped. 'All they need now is exercise.'

'Is that what the doctor told you?'

'Yes!'

She was silenced, staring at him, torn by the sight of those haggard features and the overwhelming urge to fling her arms round him.

'Why are you alone here?' she repeated, when she had control of her voice again. 'Where's Dora—and Willis?'

'That's none of your concern!'

'Then at least tell me who's looking after you!'

His brows had snapped into a fierce black line. 'Don't you think I'm capable of looking after myself?'

'Under normal circumstances—yes,' she retorted tautly. 'But you're ill, Ross. You're still not fully recovered. You need someone here——'

'I need *you* here, I suppose!' he grated. 'What's the matter, Cassie—feeling guilty? Is that why you came—to play nursemaid?'

She flinched. His voice was slashing through her like a knife, but she stood her ground, fingers still twisted tightly round her bag.

'I—I came because I couldn't go on with the way things were between us,' she got out. 'I thought that—after all this time—we could at least begin to talk to each other——'

'And what about your family?' he demanded savagely. 'Do *they* know where you are?'

She stared at him helplessly, fighting now to keep back the tears. Why was he being like this? Couldn't he see what he was doing to her? Was he still so intent on paying her back? 'I—I haven't seen my family,' she gulped. 'And besides—this has nothing to do with them——'

'On the contrary—I'd say it has *everything* to do with them!' He swung away, raking his fingers through his hair, and she was left to stare blindly at his back.

'You have every reason to be bitter——' she got out, and stopped. Oh, God—this wasn't at all what she had envisaged! It was infinitely harder than she had ever imagined—but she *had* to try and make him understand—see how she felt—why she had come. She relaxed her fingers from round her bag and lowered it clumsily on to the kitchen table, before taking a breath and beginning again.

'After—after what happened—the way my mother behaved—you had every right to do what you did,' she said, struggling to keep her voice level. 'Under the circumstances I probably would have done the same myself. I want you to know that—that I don't blame you, Ross, for what you did, and, looking back, I'm probably as much to blame as anyone.'

He was silent, staring rigidly out of the kitchen window, and she continued unsteadily, 'When you came to see me in London—I should never have sent you away, Ross. You said I'd only end up hurting myself, and you were right! That's why I had to come and see you again, to tell you how I felt. I hoped that—oh, God knows what I hoped, but I thought we would at least be able to talk!'

'There's nothing to talk about.' His voice sounded cracked, strained. 'We've been through all this before, Cassie, and nothing has changed.'

'But it has—it has!' She took a step towards him, hands outstretched in an unconscious plea. 'Events change, Ross. Our perception of events changes. And you said yourself—there's nothing that can't be overcome——'

'I was a fool—I didn't know what I was talking about!'

She swallowed painfully. 'Are you telling me, then, that I was wrong to come?'

'It would have been better if you'd stayed in London.'

'With Neil?'

Those two words had him swinging round to face her again, eyes glittering with suppressed fury. 'Damn you, Cassie, if that's why you're here—to fling McAllister in my face!'

His features told her all she needed to know. 'Oh, Ross——' she breathed, her voice tremulous now. 'You know why I've come.'

He stared at her, almost incredulously, she thought, and then, 'For God's sake, Cassie, there's nothing for you here!'

'There's you.'

He closed his eyes, as though in agony. 'You don't know what you're saying——'

'On the contrary—I've never been more sure of anything in my life. That last time—I should never have sent you away——'

'But you did! And looking back, it was the only sane thing you could have done. There can be nothing between us, Cassie!'

'Then why haven't you pressed charges against my mother?' she asked unsteadily. 'Why, Ross? I've waited, and waited—I couldn't understand it at first. And then, as the months passed—I began to hope that perhaps—after all this time——' She faltered to a halt, but he was silent, and after a moment she continued tremulously, 'I realised, too, that if you'd really wanted to hurt me that weekend, you would have told me about Julia——'

'If I'd known it would be Elaine who told you, then I *would* have done!' he broke out savagely. 'My God—when I think of what that woman has done to us——'

'Then why aren't you prosecuting?' Cassie persisted desperately.

'For heaven's sake——'

'*Why,* Ross?'

'You *know* why,' he got out at last. 'She's your mother! It would be like destroying you, Cassie. Destroying myself!'

'Oh, Ross!' She couldn't go on, could only stare at him through her tears, and then she was close to him, winding her arms round him, pressing herself against him and feeling the heat of his body melting into hers with an aching sweetness.

'Oh, God——' He could no longer resist, and she was crushed against him as his mouth found hers, fiercely passionate.

'This is madness!' he groaned, as his mouth trailed a fiery path across her cheek.

'No,' she breathed. 'It's the only sanity, Ross. At least, for me. And you feel it too, don't you? You can't deny it—not now.'

'No, I won't deny it,' he got out. 'How can I, when I've spent these last months praying for you to come— even though I knew there were a million reasons why you shouldn't——?'

'Then let me stay with you—now, tonight——'

'I can't!' He was already struggling to put her away from him, desperately trying to keep her at arm's length. 'I can't, Cassie! Why won't you understand?'

'I understand that we want each other, Ross. That we *need* each other. So why can't we be together?'

'Because we're not the only two people involved in all this——'

'We're the only two that matter!'

'And what about your grandfather?' he demanded harshly. 'Are you telling me now that *he* doesn't matter? That every time you think of him you won't think of what I did to him?'

'Ross——' she began, but he put a hand up, silencing her, holding her away from him with unsteady hands.

'No, Cassie, I know what you're trying to do, but it isn't enough! You say you want me now, but after a few months of living up here, cut off from everything, who's to say the accusations—the recriminations—won't start again? And I couldn't bear that, Cassie, not again!'

'Ross, you don't understand——'

'No, Cassie, it's you who doesn't understand,' he got out. 'There can be no future for us!'

He broke away from her to pace tautly across the kitchen, running shaking fingers through his hair. Then he began harshly, 'That weekend you came up here—the night we made love—you remember?'

She nodded, eyes darkly green, and he continued abruptly, 'Well, that night I was finally forced to admit to myself that I still wanted you. I told myself then that, despite everything, I would keep you with me—I would take what you were so blatantly offering and to hell with everything else. But you know yourself how that turned out!'

'I was unsure that day, Ross. I didn't know what to think, or feel.'

'And you're telling me that you do now?'

'I know that I love you,' she declared, 'and that we can't let what's happened in the past destroy any chance of happiness for the future.'

'And what about your grandfather's future, Cassie?' he demanded tautly. 'Are you going to tell me you can forget that? Forget the fact that he could be tied to a wheelchair for the rest of his life?'

'That has nothing to do with us.'

'But it has *everything* to do with us!' He paced restlessly back to the window. 'If I hadn't been a gullible fool and believed everything Elaine told me—if I hadn't broken every rule in the book and written those articles—my God! You said it all that night, Cassie, when you damn near accused me of libel. You made me take a long, hard look at myself, and I didn't like what I saw——'

'I had no right to say those things,' she said simply. 'Not when I only knew half the truth.'

'You don't have to make excuses, Cassie——' His face was pale now, and haggard. Tearing at her heart.

'Who's making excuses? Those articles did nothing except make me realise you were still alive!'

'I tried to destroy Brett's! I almost destroyed your grandfather——'

'You had nothing to do with my grandfather's illness,' she told him firmly, and his look was darkly intent.

'You can't be sure of that.'

'I can't be sure of it, no,' she said. 'But I do know there are other things to be taken into consideration.'

He turned back to face her, eyes narrowed. 'Such as?'

'Such as the fact that my grandfather has had a heart condition for the last four years.'

He was suddenly still, his eyes fixed on her face. 'When did you find this out?' he demanded tautly.

'Just before Christmas,' she answered. 'Neil told me.'

'McAllister?' he questioned sharply. 'You're telling me he knew and you didn't?'

'None of us knew,' she explained simply. 'Grandfather wanted it kept quiet—even from the family. Apparently only James and Sir Nigel—grandfather's doctor—did know. I went to see Sir Nigel myself. He told me that grandfather had a heart attack about four years ago; it wasn't serious, but they knew it was a warning. He was advised to retire then, but he wouldn't.' She moved her shoulders. 'So you see, it could have happened at any time. In some respects, grandfather has been lucky; he knows now that he *has* to retire, and I think, secretly, he's quite looking forward to it.' She managed a little smile. 'He's talking about buying a farm, trying his hand at breeding horses. Apparently it's something he's always wanted to do.'

But Ross didn't smile. He was still watching her, his face still pale and set, and, she thought now, deeply vulnerable.

'Why would McAllister tell you about your grandfather?' he questioned abruptly. 'That day he came here he was as mad as hell-fire. I was convinced he'd lose no time in vilifying me to all and sundry, perhaps even to the extent of persuading you to marry him at last. After all, there was never any love lost between us, Cassie. And yet he deliberately tells you something which he must have known would absolve me to some extent?'

'He could see how I was,' Cassie said without a flicker. Her face was impassive now; only her eyes were wide and bright. 'He knew how upset I was. I think he thought I was going to pine away and die for love of you——'

'Cassie!' He came to her then, winding his fingers in her hair, tilting her face up to put his lips to hers in a kiss of exquisite tenderness.

'I put you through hell,' he breathed into her hair. 'When I think of what I must have done to you that weekend—the way I behaved——' He drew a shaking breath. 'I tried to destroy you, too, and all for the sake of a——'

'No—don't say it, Ross.' She put her hand up, covering his mouth. 'What's done is done. We can't alter the past.'

'But I misjudged you, Cassie, almost as badly as I misjudged Elaine. Can you forgive me for that?'

'It's you who should forgive me,' she murmured. 'I wanted to hurt you, too, Ross. I was so confused—I didn't know what to believe any more, but these last few months I've done nothing but think about you—about us—and if I'd known you were alone up here—making a hopeless mess of looking after yourself——' She paused. 'Where are Dora and Willis, by the way?'

He had taken her hand, pressing his mouth into her palm, making her senses leap. 'Dora had a phone call to say her sister in Kendal had been involved in an accident, so she dropped everything and Willis ran her over in the Bentley. Happily, its nothing more than a few bruised ribs.' His look was smilingly speculative as his mouth moved back to hers. 'No doubt you thought I was trying to do myself to death all alone up here, hmm?'

She watched him from under her lashes. 'Something like that,' she murmured, and he grinned.

'No chance,' he told her softly. 'At least while I was alive I knew there was a chance I would see you again. Anyhow, they're coming back the day after tomorrow.'

At her look he grinned again, and then he was reaching for her, and she pressed herself against him, pushing her fingers up under his jumper, feeling the thrill of bare skin, and his body's immediate response, with a murmur of satisfaction. He was kissing her, his lips increasingly persuasive, urgently possessive, and when at last he tilted her head back to look into her face her eyes were drowsy with desire. His own eyes, too, were dark with passion, and when he looked at her now, he seemed to look through to her very soul.

'You know that if you stay with me now, it will be for ever,' he whispered unsteadily. 'There'll be no turning back, Cassie, for either of us. It'll be marriage or nothing.'

She looked at him, eyes wide and brilliantly green. 'Whatever happened to the "no commitments" clause?' she asked, innocently surprised, but he was already sliding out of his waterproof, holding her to him with one arm, before pressing her against him again and beginning to kiss her nose, her eyes, her cheeks, and anywhere else he could reach.

'To hell with no commitments!' he told her thickly. 'Aren't you at least going to take your coat off?'

Harlequin Presents

Coming Next Month

Available in January wherever paperback books are sold, or through
Harlequin Reader Service:

In the U.S.
901 Fuhrmann Blvd.
P.O. Box 1397
Buffalo, N.Y 14240-1397

In Canada
P.O. Box 603
Fort Erie, Ontario
L2A 5X3

CHRISTMAS IS FOR KIDS

Spend this holiday season with nine very special children. Children whose wishes come true at the magical time of Christmas.

Read American Romance's CHRISTMAS IS FOR KIDS—heartwarming holiday stories in which children bring together four couples who fall in love. Meet:

Frank, Dorcas, Kathy, Candy and Nicky—They become friends at St. Christopher's orphanage, but they really want to be adopted and become part of a real family, in #321 *A Carol Christmas* by Muriel Jensen.

Patty—She's a ten-year-old certified genius, but she wants what every little girl wishes for: a daddy of her own, in #322 *Mrs. Scrooge* by Barbara Bretton.

Amy and Flash—Their mom is about to deliver their newest sibling any day, but Christmas just isn't the same now—not without their dad. More than anything they want their family reunited for Christmas, in #323 *Dear Santa* by Margaret St. George.

Spencer—Living with his dad and grandpa in an all-male household has its advantages, but Spence wants Santa to bring him a mommy to love, in #324 *The Best Gift of All* by Andrea Davidson.

These children will win your hearts as they entice—and matchmake—the adults into a true romance. This holiday, invite them—and the four couples they bring together—into your home.

Look for all four CHRISTMAS IS FOR KIDS books available now from Harlequin American Romance. And happy holidays!

XMAS-KIDS-1R

Especially for you,
Christmas from
HARLEQUIN HISTORICALS

An enchanting collection of three Christmas
stories by some of your favorite authors captures
the spirit of the season in the 1800s

TUMBLEWEED CHRISTMAS by Kristin James

A "Bah, humbug" Texas rancher meets his match in his
new housekeeper, a woman determined to bring the spirit
of a Tumbleweed Christmas into his life—and love into
his heart.

A CINDERELLA CHRISTMAS by Lucy Elliot

The perfect granddaughter, sister and aunt, Mary Hillyer
seemed destined for spinsterhood until Jack Gates arrived
to discover a woman with dreams and passions that were
meant to be shared during a Cinderella Christmas.

HOME FOR CHRISTMAS
by Heather Graham Pozzessere

The magic of the season brings peace Home For
Christmas when a Yankee captain and a Southern heiress
fall in love during the Civil War.

**Look for HARLEQUIN HISTORICALS CHRISTMAS
STORIES wherever Harlequin books are sold.**

Wonderful, luxurious gifts can be yours with proofs-of-purchase from any specially marked "Indulge A Little" Harlequin or Silhouette book with the Offer Certificate properly completed, plus a check or money order (do not send cash) to cover postage and handling payable to Harlequin/Silhouette "Indulge A Little, Give A Lot" Offer. We will send you the specified gift.

Mail-in-Offer

OFFER CERTIFICATE

Item:	A. Collector's Doll	B. Soaps in a Basket	C. Potpourri Sachet	D. Scented Hangers
# of Proofs-of -Purchase	18	12	6	4
Postage & Handling	$3.25	$2.75	$2.25	$2.00
Check One				

Name _____

Address _____ Apt. # _____

City _____ State _____ Zip _____

ONE PROOF OF PURCHASE

To collect your free gift by mail you must include the necessary number of proofs-of-purchase plus postage and handling with offer certificate.

HP-3

Harlequin®/Silhouette®

Mail this certificate, designated number of proofs-of-purchase and check or money order for postage and handling to:

INDULGE A LITTLE
P.O. Box 9055
Buffalo, N.Y. 14269-9055